D1521953

NOWHERE
RUN TO

M A R K   H A N N A

Lulu Publishing Services rev. date: 02/02/2017

Contents

DEDICATION

This book is dedicated to anyone continually battling against right and wrong; against good and evil. It is also to those suffering long term physical and mental hardships or pain.

To the homeless, the past, present and future armed forces personnel and to the victims of domestic violence, I say to you all, rise up and be proud of yourself once again and what you have done, what you want to do and what you can do as today belongs to you; do not live to regret what you do not do.

This is also to my love, who always was and always will be in my heart to the end of time

X

THE REASON

There are many serving and ex-serving forces personnel that have, and continue, to place themselves at risk on a daily basis across the globe.

There are some that pay the ultimate sacrifice and others that often come back severely physically injured or psychologically scarred.

There are the lucky few that come back and merge back into society with little effort, and there are those that cannot accept the 'civvies' way of dealing with everyday life, or their lack of drive or passion.

There are others that rebel against society and target those that are perceived to be the root cause for the problems, be that an authority or the general population; these represent one in ten inmates who are ex-forces, currently in prison facilities throughout the United Kingdom.

The group we do not, or refuse, to see are those that have tried and failed, for whatever reason, to connect to an everyday existence; or those that have in extreme cases been shunned by society itself. These are the growing number of homeless ex-military personnel living on the streets of our towns and cities; the same pavements we walk on every day.

These are the people that have served across the world for our peace and security, and are now paying the sacrifice of a living hell of today. These veterans represent 1 in 3 of the homeless within the United Kingdom, often living day to day searching for food, water and the security of a safe environment to sleep without fear of bullying, harassment, hunger, illness or falling victim to extreme elements.

Although some may say that those that choose to live this way of life, know what they are getting into, but not all situations are as simple as they may first seem. Likewise this can also be true for any situation irrespective of circumstance, in which a person knows there are potential risks by doing what they do on a daily basis, be that by serving in the military, or staying in a volatile relationship.

There are over one and a half million recorded people in the United Kingdom suffering various forms of physical or psychological domestic violence, and although the majority are female, the small percentage of male abuse cannot be forgotten.

Behind the rising figures is a growing culture of acceptance towards such behaviour behind closed doors by both the perpetrators and victims, but how many others do not report it? How many others do not know where to find help? How many others are unaware that they are a prisoner of their situation and are being abused?

Struggling at the lowest levels of the physical and mental needs on the streets is only a step away from struggling to cope with a volatile relationship. Take away the basic requirements to find food, water and shelter, you still have the fear, the resentment and mental or even physical scars. These two groups of people are no different from each other, they are still suffering in different environments; but suffering nonetheless.

Joe, in this book represents those that have served, and continue to serve, our country across the world at sea, in the air, or on foreign soil. Joe is also in each and every one of us that has fallen victim to loving someone with a true passion so much it hurts.

He is one that experiences the cruel and severe life on the streets at the lowest end of the basic survival needs of all animals. Like many of us, he is a victim of circumstance and it is through Joe, we see that we should not act as a judge or jury to those victims surrounding us on a daily basis; they are already tortured enough. They know who they are. They live the hell, they experience it daily and all we can do is to be there and support them.

*Live not to judge one another and love not to
regret each other for we are soon gone*

FALLEN COMRADES

Sergeant Joe Forrester has served his country for the last 16 years and is a battle-hardened soldier with seven operational tours under his belt.

From his first tour of Northern Ireland to his last in Afghanistan, he had done his job well and has been spared the physical scars some of his colleagues now have to carry for the rest of their lives.

His battalion had lost 7 men and 23 had been severely injured in the line of duty on their last tour alone. These losses were a major blow for the 200 year old regiment, but more so for Joe, as 3 of the losses and 5 of the injured were from his own platoon.

Sabre Platoon was ambushed on the outskirts of Laskar Gah in the notorious Helmand province whilst carrying out a routine patrol as they had done so many times before. The double IED explosion combined with enemy cross-fire ensured that the patrol was not only pinned down, but endured heavy losses due to the narrowing dusty streets with little to no cover. Once the initial 'contact' report had been sent, it took more than 20 minutes for reinforcements to arrive due to another incident on the other side of the war torn town, and by the time they had re-deployed, arrived, secured and searched the area it was too late for Dave, Steve and Ron, three unfortunate victims of a deadly enemy coordinated attack.

The losses not only shook the battalion, but it sent nervous ripple waves across the remaining ISAF serving troops from those on the ground to those serving at sea. It was the worst single incident leading to losses and injuries the UK had witnessed since the invasion of the country some 12 years prior. It also led to a major change in the military approach in-country with the battle to win the hearts and minds of the population, being replaced by a hard line approach to suspected insurgents and those aiding or harboring them.

Back in the UK, all the media stations and newspapers reported the deaths and injuries as a severe blow to the morale of the troops and their families around the world. A petition was set up on the Prime Minister's own web-site and over 450,000 people had signed it within a week asking for the troops to be withdrawn immediately from Afghanistan and for the Prime Minister to resign.

A group called 'Leave Afghan Now' gathered a further 200,000 signatures and support in nearly every town and city throughout the country. Christians and Muslims alike came together to air their grievances at both the incident and at the invasion, as well as the 'hidden' political motivation for still being in a country that now had its own democratic rulers, or so the world was meant to believe.

The Prime Minister, Avril Morrison, was forced to make a statement in Parliament as well as on every national television and radio station throughout the United Kingdom, addressing the national outcry of what appeared to be a lack of political drive to return the troops from an ever increasing unstable country. It was the beginning of another Iraq.

On a cold and foggy London morning, the Prime Minister left Parliament after the initial speech and was driven under heavy armed police escort to the BBC recording studios just off of Regent Street. The Prime Minister addressed the nation in what could be the biggest challenge to her leadership to date.

"I have felt the need to address you all today regarding the tragic and sad loss and injury of our troops two weeks ago in Afghanistan.

As with all such unprovoked and cowardly attacks across the globe, we are doing everything within our power to liaise with all parties to bring those responsible to justice.

I have also been asked to resign over a failure to bring back our troops with immediate effect. However, Afghanistan is at present a country in need of our help. Not just to continue to rebuild its basic democratic society, its local, national and international businesses but to ensure it is a safe place for the local population.

Our troops as part of the International Security Assistance Force, are making small but critical steps towards such goals as well as showing the world we are leading the fight against terrorism.

The tragic lost and damaged lives of our young men and woman are a terrible cost of freedom, not just for every Afghan citizen, but for us too. It is with this in mind that I can confirm that I will not be stepping down as Prime Minister at a time when our troops, the Afghan people and our freedom and security need me to remain strong to see us through our agreed security and training plan for a country that so desperately needs our help.

Thank you for your patience, understanding and of course your support for every single man and woman that serve in our armed forces both at home and overseas."

The broadcast caused further unrest over the following weeks, with demonstrations across the country due to Morrison's apparent lack of sympathy for the loss of life and severe arrogance towards resigning. Over 360 people over the following few days of the address were arrested in cities such as Liverpool, Glasgow, London, Ipswich and Exeter and more than 100 police personnel injured in scuffles.

Not only did the demonstrations reiterate to the government that the citizens of the country had had enough of the constant losses and staggering numbers of life threatening injuries sustained by the troops on a daily basis, but politicians from all parties realised it could be a great opportunity to be seen to represent the people, especially those opposed to the Prime Minister's party. It appeared that everyone wanted to jump on the bandwagon of resistance.

Despite the politics, the public outcry and support towards the troops, it had little impact to those serving abroad; especially Joe. He felt guilty enough, not only due to the fact that he had suffered no injuries during his career, but that he was in charge of the patrol and had chosen that fateful route as they were running late for their return to base, due to an earlier issue with an abandoned vehicle they had to deal with.

It was a guilt that Joe would have to live with for the rest of his life, and one that would eventually force him to feel the need to leave the armed forces, which he had always loved with a passion.

Only those authorised by the Ministry of Defence were allowed to attend the funerals back home, and Sergeant Joe Forrester was not one of them just in case family and friends blamed him for their loss. The Commanding Officer, Regimental Sergeant Major and Sabre Platoon Commander along with 6 pall bearers from another company were dispatched to escort the union flag-draped coffins from Bagram air base to homeland soil in Oxfordshire after that slow, long and sad journey through Wooten Basset.

It was a politically motivated choice of personnel to attend the full military honour funerals and one that the remainder of the Battalion understood, but day by day, slowly but surely it ate at Joe and he began to feel more depressed at the guilt he carried.

The remainder of the tour seemed to last an eternity, and the last two months passed by without any further serious incidents. Morale was low, and the hard line tactical approach only made the situation on the ground more fragile with the locals and both the Afghan National

Police and local council leaders, refusing to pass on local intelligence or allowing extended patrols around the city without authority.

This unhealthy stance led to the withdrawal of ISAF troops from unnecessary assistance, as well as ceasing the desperately needed training of the local Afghan Army personnel. The relationship between senior personnel of ISAF and the Afghanistan President's government was also delicate and the UK Prime Minister again had to hold emergency cabinet meetings to try to avert a political storm between the two countries.

Once the agreed date was confirmed for the regiment to commence its tactical three phase return to their UK base in Victoria Barracks, morale picked up at the thought of returning to family and loved ones, as well as having some normality back in their lives. However the relationship with the locals remained strained throughout and would continue to do so for a number of months after their departure.

Joe Forrester and the remainder of his platoon departed from their operating base to Camp Bastion to embark upon their 1000 mile journey home. Joe felt a sense of loss, not just for Dave, Steve and Ron, but he was leaving a part of himself there.

He was a changed man, the tour had been so different from any of the rest, even Iraq, and he couldn't help but remember his father's words before his first operational tour.

"Son, when you come back you will not be the same person who left. A part of you will always remain there, but it is how you deal with things when you get back that makes all the difference."

HOMEWARD BOUND

The flight back for Joe was softened by the hand out of a single can of lager by the Royal Air Force flight attendants and the music playing on his iPod. Apart from the short stop off in Dubai for refueling he slept for the majority of the journey, and only woke for the on-board meals and the rare, and boring PA announcement from the pilot, whom Joe was sure only wanted to hear his own voice.

The plane landed as scheduled with the usual verbal threat about being arrested if anyone kissed the ground after departing the plane as a personal sign of being grateful to be back on UK soil.

After the normal customs and Royal Air Force Police checks, or as they are also commonly known to military personnel, snow drops due to their white hats, transport in the form of a fleet of small coaches was waiting to drive through the sunny June afternoon back to barracks.

Joe took in all of the beautiful English countryside as the coach sped along the motorway and compared it to the sporadic green lush areas of Afghanistan, as well as watching people driving by as he had done so many times in Afghanistan with suspicion.

After the last 6 months it seemed odd not having armoured vehicles and weapons at hand, and he wondered what it would be like to lead a normal life in civvie street. It was the first time he had wondered in his career what it would be like not being a soldier. He dozed off again and woke as they entered the main gates to the modernised Barracks to be met with a roar of excitement from families and the rear party colleagues that had stayed behind.

Despite the obvious joy of those with families and friends awaiting the battalion on the main parade square, Joe could not share their enthusiasm for being home. He had no parents as they had died some years previously, and only had a sister left, whom he had had little communication with over the last 10 years and an ex-wife who he didn't keep in touch with. As he watched the tears of happiness from both soldiers and families, he couldn't help but think of his sister Gaby and decided he would contact her now he was back; it had been far too long.

Joe headed to the Sergeants Mess where he had his own live-in bunk as all single mess members did.

He showered and changed into normal casual clothes rather than the multi terrain pattern camouflage clothing he had worn for his time away.

The majority of singletons went on the town to enjoy their night of freedom, and it reminded him of his first night back from his original tour when he met who was to become his wife. He smiled to himself as he wondered how many others would be in the same boat on this night, and how many would fall in love as he had.

The mess bar was open as Joe entered and sat on a stool at the end of the bar. He was met with the smiling, familiar face of Simon, the mess barman who asked in his usual cavalier way.

"Hiya Joe, how's it hanging?"

"Not too bad Simon, good to see you again, I'll have a pint of lager please."

Joe didn't really like Simon but it was always good to keep on the right side of the mess staff. The glass of beer was the best thing he had held, looked at and tasted in a long time. He closed his eyes and secretly toasted a sad farewell to his three missing friends.

He took a refill without getting into another dry-witted and boring conversation with Simon. He then went to sit at a table in the corner of the mess looking at the large regimental painting of the Battle of Alma on the opposite wall, and the regimental colours on the other.

Joe was a proud, smart and dedicated soldier, but he felt sad and lonely. He sat alone all evening apart from the barman topping up his pint on several occasions before he decided he needed a well-earned sleep and retired back to his small but adequate room. As soon as his head hit the pillow he was out like a light.

The alarm rang, which startled Joe as he jumped from the army standard issued bed and stood there for a split second before getting his bearings. He sat back on the bed, and thought it was odd not having to grab his tactical gear again.

He planned in his mind his day from having breakfast to attending the Commanding Officers talk to the battalion at 10am in the main cookhouse. It wasn't long before he was sat on the third row from the front waiting for Lieutenant Colonel Dowe to arrive.

The packed room was called to attention as the '*boss*,' as he was affectionately known by every member of the battalion, made his way to the podium.

"At ease" he ordered.

"Good morning to you all and thank you for being so prompt. I would like to start by saying how proud I am of you all for your courage, dedication and professionalism in what can only be described as the toughest and most dangerous operational deployment we have encountered to date. It is not without regret that we lost some very fine chaps whilst we were away, and I would like to try to reassure you that we are doing everything we can to liaise and support their families in every possible way. They shall not be forgotten today, tomorrow or in the future. They have shed our blood and are now part of our regimental history; they make us who we are. We will remember them" he said as he gave a small moments silence for the room to reflect.

"We will be holding a special memorial service for them in a month's time when we are all back from leave, and we hope their friends and families will join us to celebrate their lives and our loss. For the rest of us we will have to help each other with the mental and physical scars we may have. There is a programme of counseling should anyone feel the need use it, it is of course totally confidential and the number will be on every notice board throughout the barracks. I would like to finish on two key notes if I may?

The first is that I have written to the Ministry of Defence putting forward 5 people for various awards for their unselfish bravery and heroism shown throughout the tour. Once these awards have been accepted, I will make a formal announcement in due course.

The second point is that as of now you are all on annual leave as agreed with your respective company commanders, and we would like you all to try to forget the hardships we have had to endure and spend quality time with your loved ones and we will see you back here in three weeks time. May God go with you and thank you all."

In traditional form, the room was again called to attention and the Regimental Sergeant Major asked permission to dismiss the Battalion. Once the '*boss*' had left, the room was stood at ease again and the Regimental Sergeant Major piped up.

"Right, I cannot add to what the boss has said, but do not get into trouble when you're at home, I don't want to have to come and drag you out of a police cell at some Godforsaken time of the night, I won't be happy.

Remember, we are a family. We look after each other through thick and thin, and we are always there for each other. Go to your loved ones and remember that although they were not with us, they suffered you being away too. Have fun, get merry and come back refreshed and remember our regimental motto Semper Optimum; Always the best. Now go on get out of here" he said as he smiled looking at them all as though his own children were going to their first day at school; with pride yet sadness.

With that final instruction the room erupted as the battalion stormed out to start their well-earned leave.

Joe didn't have anywhere to go so he headed back to his bunk to decide what he was going to do with his time off. His private room within the mess had been his home for over three years and it was his safe area, a place where he could be himself, play his music and watch his films without fear of annoyance from anyone else, but he felt different this time.

Something was missing despite being surrounded by his personal possessions he had collected over the years. He felt soulless.

He headed back to the mess bar only to be joined by the majority of its sixty-plus members as was usual before heading off home.

Joe was never a man's man and kept himself to himself most of the time, but had on a few occasions been out with some of the lads and had one or two beers, but never too many, he always kept a level head. Joe had nowhere to go so getting drunk seemed the only thing to do, after all, he would simply fade into the background of the rest of the mess doing the same.

His only real friend, George, could not be seen through the packed bar. "Come on have another one and get me one too you tight git" Perry Matton said.

Perry was a very tall and smart character who had been in the regiment forever and was now a Drill Sergeant. For some reason he had taken a liking to Joe.

"OK Sir, one more then I'm off."

"Where the hell you going, you don't know anyone anyway."

It was a shovel to the back of the head moment as Joe thought, '*Oh my God, he's right.*'

The remainder of the night was a blur, and Joe woke the following morning to the same annoying alarm he had heard the day before, until his hand slammed down on the small travel clock ensuring it would never ring or pester him again.

Joe, in his fragile state, had a shower, got dressed then proceeded to the breakfast hall where he was served a full English breakfast and a well needed strong black coffee.

"Just what I need, thanks" he said to the sprog of a new waiter he had never seen before.

After re-fuelling himself with food and coffee, he slowly started recalling parts of the previous evening.

As he wandered back to his bunk he couldn't get out of his mind what Perry had said about not knowing anyone. He decided to contact his sister and ask if he could go and see her.

The phone rang and rang and as Joe was about to give up he heard a female voice saying hello.

"Hi it's Joe. How are you?"

"Oh my God!"

"I was wondering if I could come and see you?"

"Of course it is, are you OK?"

"Yes fine, just haven't seen you in years."

They agreed a time that day for Joe to head from Windsor up to Northolt in London where Gaby now lived.

The journey on the train and underground allowed Joe to recall the last time he saw Gaby. It was at a friend's wedding where they simply went through the niceties but they never really got on, so the chance meeting lasted less than a couple of minutes. They were always different even from his earliest memories.

Gaby was outgoing, flirtatious, had no real ambition in life and always relied on others to pull her out of trouble, the total opposite to Joe. He was nervous about meeting her again. The journey lasted just over an hour before he found himself outside of Gaby's home, a typical 1930's double storey house located in a plush part of a residential area, which was a short walk from the station.

He was in two minds to enter the small front garden when the downstairs curtain moved. It was too late, his position was compromised and he had to now make that commitment to knock at the front door. The door was opened before he could even reach for the brass knocker. Gaby had not really changed in her facial appearance, but had put some weight on, which was a good thing as she was always verging on looking anorexic in his opinion.

"Hi Joe" Gaby said as she stepped down to greet him with a tight, longing embrace.

"Hi Sis, thank you for allowing me to come over. You can let go now." Gaby released her bear hug and ushered Joe into the hallway.

"Go in the front room and I'll get some tea for us."

Joe sat in the front room and looked around at photos, ornaments and furniture and realised Gaby had a life full of her own memories and possessions. In an odd way Joe felt even more like a nomad. He had a small room with limited stuff compared to his sister's home, but then he didn't have the financial burden she had, or presumed she had.

"Here we are" she said as she entered the room with a tray packed with everything from a teapot and cups to cake, biscuits and sandwiches.

"Are we expecting others to join us?"

"Ha-ha, I thought you may be hungry. They don't really feed you properly in the Army."

"Are you sure everything's OK Joe?"

"Yes, fine really. I only got back from Afghan yesterday and thought I should make my peace between us after all these years."

"Well I am glad you have, it's been too long and it's not as though we fell out or anything. It's good to see you Joe, you look thin though."

"It's the wonderful Army diet I have to thank."

Time flew by as they chatted about everything and anything and before they knew it, it was getting dark.

"I should get going."

"Why don't you stay the night? It saves you going all the way back and there's a spare room that has not been used in ages."

Joe was feeling comfortable and thought *'why not?'*

"If you don't mind that would be great, only if I can take you for a drink somewhere to thank you?"

"No need to thank me Joe, you're my brother."

Oddly enough, Joe felt a tinge of belonging, but Perry's words still kept creeping into his thoughts.

The local wine bar was small, warming and well decorated with soft, leather chairs and occasional tables, red walls and low lighting. It felt a nice place to relax and continue chatting. Joe felt at ease with both his surroundings and his sister.

"I feel slightly lost, Gaby. I lost some good people this time and it really got to me."

Gaby listened to him without saying anything.

"I'm thinking of leaving the Army as I don't think I can handle this again."

Gaby looked shocked as she knew Joe had always wanted to be a soldier.

"Is there anything I can do?"

"Not really, it's just something I need to do, but you could help me figure out if I do leave, where I should live."

"You can always move in with me."

"I wasn't hinting, Gaby, I really wasn't."

"I know you weren't Joe. To be honest I could do with the company."

Gaby's previous relationship had broken down not long after they had moved in together, and a year later he died in a road traffic accident. His Will had never changed and his estate went to Gaby. It wasn't contested, and it allowed her to pay off the mortgage and live a fairly comfortable life, only having to take up a part-time job in the local council offices as a filing clerk.

The two bottles of dry white Chilean wine went down well and helped them both feel more at ease with each other, and Joe began to regret the loss of contact over the years.

The walk back to the house was slow as they continued to chat, and Gaby slipped her arm inside of Joe's and gave him a slight hug.

Joe was surprised at his sister and her tidiness and organisation, as she appeared to have a wonderfully clean home with everything in its place. She had everything from spare toiletries, dressing gown to slippers, as well as the great wine collection in the kitchen.

He lay on the guest bed and the wine helped his mind skip from one thought to another, from the death of his friends to how at ease he felt at Gaby's house. He soon fell asleep knowing what he had to do. He woke and checked the bedside table for his old, annoying alarm clock and then remembered he had broken it the day before.

He checked his watch and realised it was almost 9am.

He rose, and after sprucing himself up in the bathroom, felt human again and wandered downstairs. He could not hear anyone else in the house and soon found a note on the kitchen table.

'Joe, gone to work and will be back about 5pm. Help yourself to anything and spare keys to the front door are on the tag under the stairs. Have fun, Love Gaby X'

Joe was surprised but pleased that she had felt comfortable enough to trust him in her house. He wasn't as trusting with anything he owned or anyone he knew, but he felt that they were cementing the long lost brother and sister relationship they should have always had.

By the time Gaby had returned, Joe had been to the local shops and bought the brightest bunch of flowers he could find to say thank you for his sister's hospitality. He had also left a note on the reverse of hers. *'Gaby, had a really great time. Thank you and I would love to stay in touch, you have my mobile number, Love Joe x'*

Gaby felt sad Joe had left and called him straight away.

"Hi Joe, thanks for the lovely flowers and the note. If you haven't got anything to do, why not grab some stuff from the barracks and come and stay here for a while, as long as you like?"

Joe was stunned and felt wanted for the first time in a long time, and instantly agreed to return the following day.

Back in the mess, the bar was open and Joe entered and ordered a bottle of white wine. Luckily, Simon wasn't on duty so he grabbed the bottle, a glass, and sat in the small annex reading room off from the main bar.

The floor to ceiling bookcases held thousands of books from regimental history to autobiographies of every historical military leader that ever existed across the globe. It was a pleasant and quiet room with soft, leather furnishings and was often used for those studying for exams or just getting away from the hustle and bustle of every day military life. As he sat there Joe looked around at the books of Wellington, Napoleon, Genghis Khan, Churchill, Alexander the Great, Caesar, Cromwell, Attila the Hun, Eugene of Savoy, Von Clausewitz, Hannibal, Rommel and Ney and felt overwhelmed to be sitting in the same room as so many great leaders in their own right, he also realised that he was never going to shake the military world as these, and so many more had done, and although all of them had lost men under their command, his sense of guilt outweighed his pride of remaining to serve his country.

No matter how much he fought with himself he believed he had let the regiment down. The regiment he so passionately defended. The regiment he would have died for. He knew he had to leave.

He could not face remaining as he was constantly surrounded by memories of the blood on his hands, or those that had been injured, let alone allowing himself to become paranoid of people talking about him, especially Ron's wife, Tina. She surely had to hate him for what had happened.

He remembered Ron and Tina and how they had lavishly entertained their friends despite being a junior rank. They were both lovely people and were a fantastic couple madly in love. He had changed all that overnight with a bad military decision.

'Why did he have to go down that street? Why did he let this happen and what would all of these leaders around him have thought?' he questioned.

They say that there are two types of tactical decisions. One that works called good military judgement, and one that doesn't called a failure, such as Custer's last stand in 1876. The 1812 French invasion of Russia, the 1836 disaster at the Alamo, the Gallipoli invasion in 1915, the German invasion of Russia in 1941, and oddly enough the Russian invasion of Afghanistan in 1979 amongst others. The second bottle of wine blurred Joe's memory and helped him to forget as he slowly slipped into a state of oblivion.

Joe was woken by Duty Piquet Sergeant, Steve Dakin. Steve was a colleague who knew him well and had served with him for the last few years in both Iraq and Africa.

Steve slowly shook his arm. "Joe, come on mate we're closing the mess."

Steve led Joe to his bunk and placed him on his bed in the recovery position, as was normal with intoxicated people to ensure he didn't swallow his tongue or choke on his vomit overnight.

Joe's eyes slowly started functioning to get his room into focus the following morning. The shot of pain in his head made him realise he was going to suffer for last night's drinking session as he slowly clambered off of his bed and realised he was still fully dressed.

'*What the hell happened to me?*' he thought. He didn't like to be out of control.

Breakfast in the mess was again the same old same old and he soon found himself remembering he had promised Gaby he would head back over there. Although he didn't feel up to the trip back into the rat race of London, he didn't want to let her down now that they had re-kindled the relationship they had both wished for over the years. He left on the 11:05 train to London.

Joe spent the strangest week of his life in Northolt. It was a different world with no agenda, no instructions and no rigid food regimes. He could wear what he wanted and come and go as he pleased.

Gaby was relaxed with him being there and it was the first time in his life he had enjoyed being on leave. He didn't have to worry about what others thought and he didn't have to rely on others to watch his back.

Gaby and Joe became not just brother and sister again but friends, going out daily for lunch, dinner and drinks whenever they wanted, but Joe always kept an eye on everyone in the room. He trusted no-one outside of his team, but for the first time in his adult career, Joe felt as relaxed as he could around civvies. Joe missed his friends and the close ties they all had built up over the years.

THE ROCK CLIMBER

J oe decided it was time to head back to camp not just to replenish his limited clothing, but in a strange way he missed the comfort and security of the barracks and what and who he knew.

It was good walking back through the gates and waving to the familiar faces of the barrack guard on duty as if to say, *'I've missed you all.'*

Joe took lunch in the mess and after ordering his favourite meal of ham, eggs, chips and beans he then made his way through the ghost town of a barracks to the chapel at the other end of the parade square commandeering the centre of the camp.

Joe had never been a religious person but always felt a sense of peace in the chapel, even at the compulsory attendances. So much so he once had to read out a passage from The Bible at a Remembrance Day service which he was later congratulated for by the Commanding Officer.

He still remembered and recalled the passage to himself when he felt down, and although it did not comfort him he now felt it was fate after losing close friends.

1 Thessalonians 4:13-14

But we do not want you to be uninformed, brethren, about those who are asleep, that you may not grieve, as do the rest who have

no hope. For if we believe that Jesus died and rose again, even so
God will bring with him those who have fallen asleep in Jesus.

He sat in the chapel thinking about that fateful day in Afghanistan and wishing he had chosen another route. He felt the guilt every second of the day.

He thought about those seriously injured since the beginning of the conflict and considered himself lucky, and although he had some minor scars from Iraq and Northern Ireland he felt guilt for those that had, and still were, paying the ultimate price of being a soldier.

He remembered the history of the regiments' battles from the English Civil War, Waterloo, Flanders through to Iraq; the losses had been in the hundreds of thousands.

Although he knew he had wanted to join the Army since he was eight years of age, and knew the potential consequences of going into battle, he now knew he didn't want to be added to that never-ending list of fallen comrades.

He knew it was only a matter of time before it was his turn, but he also knew he had to leave everything he had ever hoped and wished for; a life in the Army.

He headed back to the mess bar for some comfort in a bottle of wine.

Joe was still in the bar when the sun set. He checked his watch, it was nearing 10pm, and feeling morose he sat outside waiting to listen to the nightly bugle call of last post. He often did this when he felt low and it made him think of the past, but never the future.

The bugle call had a major historical meaning. It was first used to indicate to troops that the battle for the day had ended and those injured would follow the bugle call to find their way back to safe lines. It was saying it was a military day done.

The duty drummer raised his brass bugle and warmed the mouthpiece. The first low note came out and the drummer played with emotion as he played the most haunting rendition Joe had ever heard.

Joe could not think of anything else apart from his own memories he carried around with him, yet for Joe, it stood for peace, for eternal hope and it was a time for a soldier to close his eyes and remember who he is, where he has come from, and what he has sacrificed.

It was a sad time as he knew tomorrow would change the rest of his life.

He woke late, but then again he had nothing to get up for. He still had almost another two weeks of leave left, but all he could think of was the task in hand.

The orderly room was quiet as usual on a leave day, but the duty Orderly Officer was perched at his desk pretending to be busy, and shoved a Sudoku puzzle book in his drawer as Joe entered.

"Morning Sir" Joe said as he stood to attention.

"Morning Sergeant Forrester. Why are you not at home?"

"This is my home Sir. I need to ask for your advice if I may?"

"I would like to formally request a termination of my service."

"You know that it will take a year, don't you?" Lieutenant Sandwell replied.

"Yes sir, I do but I need to get the notice in now."

"I understand, but you are one of the most experienced soldiers we have."

"I appreciate that Sir, but I have to think about the rest of my life." The forms were eventually found and signed by both parties and Joe walked away from the orderly room with a sense of guilt and pride. He felt guilty that he was letting his colleagues down, but at the same time he felt a sense of pride as he needed to do this for himself, and his own sanity and survival.

He had always done things for other people, always for his country but this time it was for him alone.

Joe wandered back across the parade square, knowing that if the Regimental Sergeant Major caught him, he would get the rifting of his life as the *'square'* was hallowed ground and important to his regiment's pride and discipline.

He walked over it thinking how many people had marched on it, and again remembered the regimental motto *'Semper Optimum'*.

He had always tried to be the best. He had always strived to get away from the council estate stigma he was brought up with, and he had dedicated his life to his new family, the regiment he loved with a passion and one he dedicated his life to.

Joe called Gaby and explained what he had done.

"Are you sure that's what you want?" she asked with a voice of uncertainty.

"Yes it's been playing on my mind for a long time now. Now is the right time."

"OK as long as you know what you're doing. What will you do when you leave?"

"God knows, I haven't though that far ahead yet."

Joe really hadn't thought that far in advance but he needed to. His military experience and area of expertise with explosives, sniping and close observation may not be exactly what civvie employers were looking for, unless he wanted to head back to Iraq, Afghanistan or even Syria for a specialised security company, but not having to go back into a conflict zone was the main reason he was leaving the Army.

Joe headed into town for a change of scenery and some real pub grub. The mess food was OK but it sometimes felt as if no matter what you ordered, you were eating the same as you had last time.

The Kings Arms was always welcoming, with a warm atmosphere and a rather bubbly landlord by the name of Steve, and some great traditional food. His wife Maureen had previously had an affair with one of Joe's platoon members but her husband found out, and apart from threatening to kill him he simply approached the Commanding Officer and formally complained.

Although there was very little the Commanding Officer could do, he did have a quiet word with the Private and after a few weeks of keeping away from the pub, life went back to normal, but the landlord kept a very close eye on his wife and who she was talking to or paying too much attention to.

She was a nice looking woman and she knew it and loved the attention. Joe had seen many Maureen's in his time and he knew she would have affairs throughout their relationship.

"Hi Joe" Steve said.

"Hi Steve, how's business?"

"Not too bad, it's been quiet since you guys have gone on leave."

"I know the barracks is dead, it's great for some peace for a change from the normal rat race."

"So how come you're not heading away?"

"Been to my sisters already and came back as there was something I needed to do." Steve nodded in acknowledgement and left to tend to another customer sitting at the bar.

Joe had always liked a barmaid that worked there, but had never said anything apart from the usual inane greetings. Julia was a quiet, beautiful woman who didn't know how gorgeous she was.

Joe loved it on the occasions she was on duty in the bar. He loved her blue-flecked eyes and the way she looked at him, but nothing was ever said. He loved the way she stared at him when they spoke and it seemed as though he could see into her soul through her eyes.

He wasn't the sort of man to show his emotions easily, plus she was married, and from what he could make out by her body language, she wasn't happy in her relationship but tried to cover it well. Joe knew people and could sense there was something there but he didn't know if she even noticed him let alone liked him.

Joe liked the mess bar, it was cheap, open nearly all the hours there were in a day and it was a cosy and peaceful place at times. The Kings Arms however gave something that the mess couldn't. Atmosphere, and of course it had Julia.

In the pub, Joe liked to sit in the small bay window as he could see the whole bar and the main door as well as watching locals and tourists wander past seeing the sights of the town.

Joe was a people watcher, he always had been and he could judge people well. He needed to at times, especially when on deployment.

Joe sat there for a few hours in his own world and thought of life's ifs and buts. He thought about his failed marriage and how his wife had been seeing someone behind his back for so long, and how he didn't even know about it, yet everyone else in the battalion did!

He noticed Julia enter the bar and a smile came across his face as he watched her as she prepared herself for the shift.

She was as beautiful as always wearing her usual black, smart clothing.

'My God, she's coming over here' he thought as he started to panic.

"Hi Joe, how are you today?" she said as she lifted his empty glass from the table.

Joe could have died on the spot, his heart was racing and he could hardly speak. He stood up out of natural instinct.

"Hi Julia, err you on shift today then?"

'What a prat!' he thought to himself and he could have slapped himself for being so stupid.

"Very observant" she said as she simply laughed sensing Joe's embarrassment.

"If you need anything, just let me know."

Joe could feel his face going red. He really wanted to ask her to sit with him, to get to know her. Just to be with her.

Joe sat and as he continued secretly watching her, he was sure she kept looking in his direction. *'Come on get a grip'* he thought.

He eventually plucked up the courage to head to the bar for another drink.

"Missed me already?"

My God, could he say yes?

"Of course, always" he said with a nervous laugh.

"Can I have a large glass of white wine please?"

"Of course you can."

"You not heading anywhere tonight?"

"No just relaxing and watc..." he quickly stopped himself from saying anything further.

'Idiot, you nearly gave the game away' he thought again.

He was about to say watching you, but Julia simply smiled at him and as she placed the glass in front of him and their fingers touched for the first time.

Joe felt a shivering sensation go through him. He had touched her! His heart was off again as though it was racing around his body screaming with joy inside, but no one could hear it apart from him.

"Sorry."

Julia simply touched his forearm. "Never apologise, Joe."

He was surely now having a heart attack. He was red-faced, his heart was beating and he wanted to kiss her. He nervously went back to the bay window not knowing how his legs carried him.

He needed to calm down. He had been in some sticky situations around the world and yet he couldn't handle chatting to Julia in a public place.

'Remember she's married' he thought.

Steve came wandering over.

"Sorry about earlier, where were we?"

"We were saying how quiet it was."

"Aha, that's right, but glad to have your company in here Joe as always."

"Thanks, I have always liked coming in here, it's a great place you run."

"I can see Julia has a thing for you too" Steve surprisingly revealed. Joe nearly choked on his wine.

"What!"

"Come on Joe, open your eyes man, she's a lovely woman."

"But she's married."

"Only on paper" Steve said as he plonked himself down next to Joe and he began to tell Joe all about Julia's life.

She had been married for over 26 years, had a couple of kids. She was living in a loveless relationship.

"You're the one person she likes talking to, Joe; want me to put in a good word for you?"

"God no!"

"I was only kidding. Anyway enjoy your evening, and of course the view" Steve said as he headed back towards the bar touching Joe on the shoulder as a father would a son.

Joe was paranoid that Steve would say something to Julia, he was a warm character and always wanted to help people. This was one time he didn't need his help.

He didn't want to go back to the bar, but his glass was empty, the fastening heart rate and shock of Steve's comments made him gulp the remainder of the wine down far too quickly.

Dilemma time; Should he leave or stay? He didn't like being out of control in any situation, especially with his emotions.

He headed to the bar whilst Julia was in the back, but as he arrived, she appeared as if by magic.

"Same again Joe?"

Before he could stop himself, he started talking. "Yes please and can I get you a drink too?"

'What the hell did I just say?' he questioned himself.

"Ahh that would be lovely thank you. I have a break in about 20 minutes, can I take it then please?"

"Absolutely, please do."

Returning to his table, he couldn't get her gorgeous eyes out of his thoughts, she was so beautiful and had the softest, gentlest character he had known in any person.

'I wonder where she takes her break' he thought.

Joe felt attracted to her more and more each time he saw her. There was a magnetic pull towards her irrespective of his mental objections.

He watched her leave the bar on her break and head to a chair near him. She raised her glass as if to say thank you.

Without hesitation he pointed to the chair at his table gesturing for her to come and join him if she wanted too.

'My God, she was coming over, I didn't really think she would' he thought as he stood to greet her again. "Thank you for the drink."

"It's my absolute pleasure."

Immediately, for some strange reason, Joe felt at total ease with having her so close by despite his cautions and he loved listening to her and watching her.

It seemed like only seconds before Julia had to go back to work. "Thank you again Joe, and next time, please let me buy you one."

His mouth ran off with him again.

"Only if it can be away from here though?"

"I'd like that" she said as she left the table.

What had he done he wondered. *'I think I just asked her out!'*

He was going against all of his natural instincts. She was married. He didn't want a relationship. She was at work, and he was a customer.

She was stunning though, and he kept on remembering her beautiful, capturing eyes and he loved the way she spoke and what she said. *'God, the good outweighed the bad'* he thought, as he battled with his own feelings.

It was time for Joe to leave before he got too hammered and said something to Julia which would either be embarrassing for her, or inappropriate for him.

He bid them all farewell and stood at the bar.

"Here's one for the road" Steve said, as he handed him another glass of wine.

"Blimey, thanks Steve, please let me pay for it though?"

"Not at all man. I own the place and I think I'm allowed to get my friend a drink."

"Then thank you sir, here's to your health." He lifted the glass to toast his host.

"See, I told you she liked you. You two were getting along fine over there."

"We were just keeping each other company that's all."

"You make a good couple Joe, you really do." Again Joe almost spat out his drink.

"Only pulling your leg" Steve said as he slapped him on the arm and walked off.

Joe was in his own world thinking about the time at the table, and then Julia appeared.

"You OK, Joe?"

"I am thank you; I am sure wine when it's free tastes much better."

"Sometimes it's the company you're with too."

Joe just stared at her not knowing what to say. "Are you working tomorrow night?"

"I am. Will you be in here too Joe?"

"I will be."

"Same table same time?" she said as she smiled.

'What did that mean?' he thought. Was he going to sit at the same table or was she referring to her joining him again. Either way, he was going to be there. How could he not?

"Good night" he said as he headed to the door.

Before he got to the main entrance, he looked around and caught Julia's stare and he almost walked into the door. He looked at her and slapped his head as if to say *'I'm an idiot'* but she laughed and gave him a wonderful smile. He left feeling warm inside.

The walk back to the barracks was only five minutes and Joe started to think what it would be like to live as a civvie. To shop, drink, eat and sleep like one, and of course having a proper relationship, not one based around a camp.

For the first time in a long time, he felt good, he forgot about military life and his bad experiences and nightmares.

Joe lay on his bed thinking of Julia and how stupid he had been. *'What does she think of me now'* he wondered. He hoped that she didn't think of him as a typical squaddie. He wasn't. He never had been. He liked his own company and wasn't 'one of the boys.' He fell asleep a happy man.

Late the next morning he woke and decided to call Gaby.

"Hi Gaby it's me, Joe. Hope your OK? I know we said about meeting soon, but I need a few days back in the barracks as there is something I need to do" he said to the voicemail recording.

"I will call in a few days' time - take care." He hung up the phone.

After eating what felt like a bland mess brunch after a heavy night of drinking, Joe headed back into town and casually looked in the shops before finding a small coffee shop.

It was too early for Julia to start work, so he needed to waste time in the hope of catching her before she entered the pub.

It was just before 2pm when Joe decided to head to the Kings Arms. As he walked towards the door, a car pulled up and he could see Julia in the passenger seat. She leaned over and kissed a man who he presumed was her husband.

Joe felt awkward and he reached the door just before she did and held it open as she entered. Julia scuffled through the door not even acknowledging him.

"Joe. Good afternoon to you" Steve said indicating to a bottle of wine.

Steve poured the glass and handed it over. Joe paid and headed to his usual viewing table.

A few minutes later Julia appeared and walked towards Joe.

"I am really sorry, Joe. I didn't mean to ignore you when I came in. My husband doesn't like me to chat to anyone. Odd considering that I work in a bar, don't you think?"

"Please don't apologise, I understand."

"I am sorry if I embarrassed you."

"You could never do that, you're too lovely" she said with that beaming smile.

There it went again, Joe's heart started pounding. Joe sat there in complete shock. *'How could I respond to that'* he thought! He either needed to leave her alone and forget his ideas, or tell her he liked her too.

A couple of hours went by and Joe didn't notice Julia come over to the table as he was reading the local paper.

"Boo! It's me. Mind if I join you again?"

"I would love you too."

They sat chatting about everything and nothing and eventually Joe plucked up the courage to ask what he had wanted to all along.

"Julia, I really hope you don't mind me asking, but were you serious about having a drink away from here?"

"I am Joe yes; it's just difficult with being married."

"I do understand and I hope you don't mind me asking."

"I am very flattered and would love to spend more time with you, you make me feel at ease and I love chatting to you."

How he didn't burst with happiness, he didn't know, but he was doing well and had not said anything stupid. Yet!

Again the break was up far too soon, and Joe stood as Julia rose from the chair.

"I really like you, Julia."

"I really like you too" she responded as she touched his arm gently, just above his wrist and walked towards the bar.

'*My God, my God, my God*' he kept thinking. Joe's head was all over the place. He looked at the bar as he approached and saw Maureen watching him.

"Can I have another glass of wine please?"

"Of course you can, Joe dear. Be careful with Julia, remember what happened to me. You really don't want her husband on the war path."

"I will. Thank you."

What was her husband like? What was his name? Where did she live? So many questions he wanted to ask, but all very private he thought as he headed back to the table.

Over the next few days, he repeated his routine seeing Julia as much as he could. They were getting on well and it seemed as though they were not worried about the pub's surroundings, or who was in there, but Joe always made sure he knew who was in the bar, and who was watching.

Despite being careful, it was obvious to anyone there that there was lots of laughter and flirting. Pure chemistry could be seen between the two of them as only true lovers know.

Steve had deliberately told Julia to take longer breaks. Steve liked them both and although he said it in jest, they did make a good couple, albeit a couple who could never be.

It was on one of their nightly meetings that as Julia went to rise from the chair, Joe leaned forward.

"I would love to kiss you right now."

Julia looked at him. "God, me too Joe, but we can't."

"I know sorry."

She touched his face softly with her hand, smiled and headed back to the bar. Joe had lost all of his inhibitions with Julia and had forgotten, or wanted to forget that she was married. He wanted to spend more and more time with her and he knew he was falling in love with her as he had never done before.

Joe knew nothing could ever happen between them. It wasn't his style and he really didn't want to get into a relationship with a married woman and all the potential trouble that can come along with it.

Joe really liked Julia and it was obvious she liked him too, he had found a friend. A friend he wanted to know more about in every way.

Joe ordered his final drink of the evening.

"Julia, I am sorry about before, I shouldn't have asked."

"Oh Joe, it's fine, I wish I could, but my husband would go mental if he knew I was even talking to you."

"Friends?"

"Of course, I would like that" she replied as she laid her hand on his.

Joe leaned forward and kissed her hand. After all, the bar was dead, and it felt so right to do.

Joe woke the next morning and felt guilty about spending so much time back in the barracks, or more precisely the Kings Arms. He called Gaby and explained he would come up for the last few days of his leave. He spent the last evening in the Kings Arms for a while, sitting there watching Julia during what had become their ritual meeting, nothing more was mentioned about the drink or kiss. They were now friends, but Joe was disturbed after she had told him about her home situation and how controlled her life was.

Joe could only listen. He couldn't offer her any light at the end of the tunnel, or a way out. He could only wish he could whisk her away, but he needed to remember not to breach that boundary between friends and enter the minefield of a shared relationship. He also knew in his heart she wouldn't, or couldn't, leave.

Although he was disappointed for her, he understood, after all, he had been working and living in a controlled environment for the last 16 years. Their feelings for each other were not mentioned again.

The remainder of his leave was spent going back and forth to Gaby's and building on their long lost relationship, and occasionally drinking and chatting to Julia in the Kings Arms.

It was going well with Gaby and they both liked each other's company. It was during one of his visits to his sisters that Gaby suggested he could rent a room from her once he left the Army. At least he had accommodation sorted if he needed it, but he wanted to make it on his own rather than relying on charity from his own sister but he never told Gaby that.

It was his pride, his personal drive for excellence which he had always strived to achieve, but to some he was seen as independent, or a loner. It didn't help that on some of his leave in the past he had packed his Bergen and headed off camping, hill walking or climbing.

He enjoyed the outdoors and it didn't bother him what the weather conditions were like, he saw it as a challenge. It was a good job considering what he was going to encounter.

After the regiment's leave had finished, life in the non-operational military role commenced with ceremonial duties. At least as a Sergeant, Joe had the luxury of spending the majority of the time in the guard room, rather than the junior ranks who stood guard in sentry boxes at Windsor Castle, St James Palace or Buckingham Palace.

Although they were proud moments, and working together in a smart, coordinated manner looked so good in their finest, world-renowned, scarlet coloured uniforms, Joe was definitely an outdoor person and preferred the field rather than the parade ground, but both were essential to the discipline which ran as the back-bone to every regiment in the British Army.

As weeks turned into months, Joe continued to give the same 100% dedication as he had always applied to everything he had put his mind too. Inside however, he knew he needed to change to adapt to civilian life, and both Gaby and Julia had helped him realise that, as well as showing him there are more important things than being a soldier.

He was a loner, and had few friends in or out of the Army and he had learnt to enjoy his own company and experience many of life's wonders. He was not afraid to be alone.

The last few months of Joe's service soon came around and meetings with a variety of people took place. From the Resettlement Information Officer to the Joint Service Housing Advice Organisation's representative, he felt bombarded with information and help, there was just so much to take in which seemed to be irrelevant. All of this seemed alien to someone who was used to doing things on his own and not asking for help.

Joe had joined young, had no experience outside of the military and now he had to think about a new career, what resettlement option he wanted and where to live. At least Gaby had given him one get out clause regarding his accommodation, from the spiraling list of things being thrown his way.

The process of leaving was coming to an end and after agreeing to take the generous resettlement training cost grant, and opting out of the employment support programme which could have seen him being assisted in gaining employment, he knew he had to have a mental strategy for exiting the only stable thing he had in his life.

With so much time accrued during his resettlement period, he had spent a lot of time at Gaby's, and had finalised the agreement to rent the room from her. At least it gave him a base to begin with.

He had also contacted a local security company and after a pathetic interview, had secured a low level security officer position. It was OK for now until he could get something better, a real job he thought. He used the grant to attend a legally required government training course, needed to gain a license to work in contract security and spent more time in the Kings Arms and less in the mess which had served him well, as he needed to become civilianised. Chatting to Steve, Maureen and, of course, Julia gave him the pros and cons of living a normal life outside of her Majesty's armed forces.

In true regimental style, the Sergeants Mess put on a leaving do for Joe in the form of a few drinks in the bar. Joe had always made it clear to his superiors that he didn't want any fuss when he left. Others had, in the past, been given strippers, trips or been taken out to a chosen venue. Joe had simply asked the Regimental Sergeant Major if he could bring some guests in for some drinks. It was agreed, and although he was admired in the regiment, many thought of him as odd for not wanting a '*proper military style*' send off.

His invite to Steve and Maureen had been accepted, and although he had invited Julia he didn't expect her to turn up, which although disappointed him, he understood.

The evening soon came and a call from the guard room to the mess came through stating that his guests had arrived. Joe left the bar and headed to meet them at the main gates. His heart jumped as he saw Julia standing there with Steve and Maureen. He couldn't help but smile to himself as he walked nearer.

"Really good to see you all" Joe said.

What really went through his mind was that it had made his night seeing Julia, and he couldn't stop looking at her as he escorted them under the archway and to the mess bar. It was tradition for the leaving member of the mess to buy a drink, and as such, the usual scroungers as well as those that liked Joe were in attendance.

As they entered Joe took Maureen and Julia's coats. As Julia slipped off her coat, he saw her smooth shoulders and so desperately wanted to kiss her. She looked stunning, more stunning than ever before in her long, black dress and her elegant silver jewelry. He couldn't take his eyes off of her.

As guests were not allowed to buy drinks, Joe ordered the drinks for everyone.

Joe leaned over to Julia.

"I didn't think you would make it."

"I told him I was being taken out by Steve and Maureen for a works do."

"You have made my year by coming."

They looked at each other and they knew they wanted, and had to have, each other so desperately.

The time came when The Regimental Sergeant Major called for order in the bar, and Joe knew he was about to be embarrassed.

"Sergeant Forrester, please come and join me" he said in his booming, commanding voice and Joe stood next to him as he continued talking. "For those that know Joe, he has been the back bone to this battalion since the day he joined. He has served her Majesty, this regiment, this battalion, and each and every one of us with dedication, professionalism and courage. He has served around the world, seen more than most, made and lost friends, and more importantly, he still remains a humble man. I wish we had more people like Joe in the Army."

Joe could feel himself blushing and started looking down at the floor as he knew all eyes were on him, especially Julia's.

"You will be sorely missed, my friend, and it took us a long time to know what to get you, but eventually we decided to get something that would remind you of your days with us and doing something you loved."

A mess orderly marched into the room and halted in front of them both. A stunning, silver statue of a climber perched on the side of a rock with a small engraving was handed over.

"Joe, we know you love being outdoors so much, we once thought you were a hermit. Please accept this gift in the manner it is intended. You have always climbed to reach the summit of your chosen rock and always inspired others to do the same. Well done Joe, and remember, when we mature and leave our family environment, we always remain a part of that family. Just because you're not here, it doesn't mean you're not missed."

The gift was handed to Joe as the mess erupted with cheers and clapping.

"Come on Joe, speech" was shouted from the back of the room by his old friend George.

The Regimental Sergeant Major stepped back to allow Joe his minute of fame. The Army taught you to speak with confidence and to present yourself impeccably, despite any embarrassment you may be feeling.

"Wow, I'm a bit lost for words. I cannot thank you enough, not just for the wonderful gift which I will always cherish, but for everything this regiment has taught me. For my friends and for the experiences we have shared together. I would also like to thank Steve and Maureen for coming tonight and of course, Julia for making it so special." Julia smiled lovingly at Joe.

"I am sure I will get to talk to you all before I leave, and once again, thank you for coming."

Joe headed back to the security of his table passing through the crowd and getting pats on the back and handshakes.

His guests stood up to meet him back at the table. Steve shook his hand and Maureen kissed him on the cheek. As he turned to Julia, she cupped his face with her hands and kissed him on the lips. His stomach felt as though it was doing summersaults as he felt her soft, warm lips.

"Well done, Joe."

Joe was stunned. He couldn't say anything as he stared into her gorgeous eyes. Steve raised his glass.

"You'll always have somewhere to stay at the Arms Joe, cheers." Joe for the first time in his life felt sad. He was leaving the regiment, the people he knew, the only life he knew and of course, Julia.

After a short while, Steve stood up.

"Right mate, we're off, but Julia wants to stay for a while, and please look after her with this pack of wolves" he continued, referring to what happened previously with his wife.

Joe was stunned again, making it too many times in one evening. "Are you OK with that, Julia?"

"I am Joe, I would love to stay longer."

Joe walked them to the main doors and watched as they headed towards the gates arm in arm.

He returned warm-heartedly to Julia patiently sitting there.

"I am really glad you stayed."

"Me too Joe, but I can't stay out too long."

With the constant interruptions from well-wishers, Joe asked Julia if she wanted to move into the peace and quiet of the annex room. Julia was mesmerised with the room with its splendor.

"This is an amazing room, I can see you sit in here a lot."

"I do, it allows you to think and hardly anyone uses it."

They sat next to each other on one of the leather sofas facing the wall of books.

"You look absolutely stunning, Julia."

"Thank you, you look the same, I love the red jacket and medals, what are they for?"

"Oh various bits of metal the Army didn't want any longer."

In reality, he was proud of every one of them and what he had done, but he was not one for talking about himself.

"I will miss you when you go."

"Me too Julia, I have come to really, really like you, and enjoy seeing and chatting to you whenever I can, about anything."

"I told you we would have that drink somewhere away from the Arms."

They laughed and then looked at each other with pure passion and leaned forward as their lips gently and softly touched.

The tingling sensation ran through their bodies as they knew they wanted each other. They kissed again and embraced.

"God, I want you" Julia said.

Joe stood and held his hand out and as Julia took it, he led her away. Joe unlocked his room and let Julia enter with no words being said, the door was closed. Words could not express how much they felt for each other or how much they wanted to feel each other.

SOMEONE NEEDS YOU

J oe left through the barrack gates for the last time. It was a sad feeling, but a step he needed to take for himself. He looked back through the archway to the drill square and the mess in the distance. So many memories, so many experiences and so many mess bills! He had always remembered what his friend Simon had told him some years before when he himself had left.

"Remember all the crap things about the Army. Those are the things that will keep you from going back."

As Joe sat on the train heading into London, he remembered some of the bad times, army slang and of course those he had seen lose their lives or been disfigured for life. He now knew what Simon had meant. The feeling of guilt that it had not been himself, or that gut-wrenching feeling that he had caused some of the heartache now inflicted upon others.

For the first time in his life he felt ashamed, guilty and alone. It was a sad day for a proud ex-soldier who had surrendered his life to serving Queen and country.

Gaby had taken the day off work to meet Joe when he arrived at her home.

"Welcome home" she said as she greeted him at the door.

"The room is all freshly made up and ready if you want to throw your stuff up there first."

"Thanks, Sis, be back in a minute."

Joe put the bags and Bergen on the floor, sat on the small chair in the corner and tried to take in the whole aspect of having left everything he knew behind.

He thought of Julia and his only night with her. He did not regret giving her his parting gift of the rock climber statue he was presented and although he knew she couldn't take it home, it sat well on the shelf behind the bar in the Arms. At least she could always look at it and think of him, as he would when he looked at the photo he had taken of her laying in his bed. He would always be there for her no matter what she needed, no matter what had happened or how much time had elapsed.

Gaby was secretly pleased her brother had left. No more having to watch the TV to see if he had been one of those injured or killed. No more worrying and no more wondering what he was doing. She had him back where he belonged. She had already placed a bottle of champagne on chill and two flutes were heard clinking as he entered the living room.

"Well, that's that done, another chapter of my life begins." They toasted each other and Joe's new chosen path in life.

The following few weeks at his new home allowed him to settle in before he had to report for his new job. How odd he felt in his new environment, no need to get up early, prepare his kit and no need to answer to anyone. Life seemed completely opposite to what he had been used to for so many years.

Gaby had made him feel welcome from day one. She had ensured he had wanted for nothing and she enjoyed having him at her home. She enjoyed their many chats in which they both seemed to open up their hearts. Joe told her about his experiences, his thoughts and fears as well as the reasons he left the Army he loved so much.

He eventually told her about how much he secretly loved Julia and about the situation. Gaby in return told him about her turbulent relationship with her long term boyfriend Mac, and how he seemed to know the right triggers to set her off on the spiral path of aggression. She also discussed in detail the night she threw him out and how she had picked up a cup and hit him heavily cutting his head. She explained how she hated the violence, but he pushed her to it every time.

Joe felt uneasy listening to his sister's dark side and remembered one of his colleagues had come to work one day with a fractured hand. They all knew his wife was capable of such things, but no-one believed she would stoop to such a low level. She did, and although everyone knew he should have left her, he stayed. At least Gaby had called it a day either through guilt or frustration. That way it couldn't escalate any further; it was unfortunate that he later died.

Gaby would often return home to prepared dinners and a bottle or two of wine set at the table. This is something she liked but rarely had done for herself in the past. Joe enjoyed doing it, he had always liked cooking for himself, he felt happy and comfortable in the kitchen and wished he could have been doing it for someone, for Julia.

Joe would sometimes get a call asking him to join his sister in a local bar or with her work friends, and wondered if she was trying to pair him off with one of the young females of her team, as she would often introduce him and them wander off. It was on one of these invites that he had arrived early and sat himself in a quiet corner overlooking the rest of the room when he deiced to call the Arms.

"Hi Steve. It's Joe."

"God, hi you, it's great to hear from you, how's it all going?"

"I'm OK thanks, feels odd, but OK. How's Julia?"

"I take you have not heard?"

"No what's happened?"

"She was beaten up by her old man."

"What! What the fuck did he do that for?"

Steve explained that she had said to her husband that she had enjoyed her work's night out. He had been drinking and had laid into her physically, and as a consequence she had suffered some serious bruising.

Joe was fuming, and agreed with Steve that he would come and visit them to discuss it in more detail, and stay for a few days.

Gaby rolled into the bar some time later to find Joe agitated.

"Gaby, I am really sorry, I may have to head back to Windsor for a while."

Gaby could sense something was wrong. She had already had a few drinks at work and in another bar before meeting him. Joe could smell the alcohol on her breath and knew she was half way to being plastered. He didn't want to inject fuel to the fire.

"What's happened?" she asked.

"It's Julia, she's been beaten up by her old man."

"That's what you get when you're seeing someone who's married."

Joe was shocked. She had always been so understanding of his feelings towards Julia, and this really took him by surprise. He wanted to grab her, but he knew he wouldn't.

"I really can't believe you said that after everything I have told you" he replied with anger in his voice.

"Come on, Joe, have a drink with us, she'll be OK. They always are! Anyway, you should concentrate on your new life now, not the past."

Joe started seeing red and snapped back.

"Are you serious, this is not Mac we're talking about, it may be OK in your world to slap someone around, but it's not in mine or in any normal persons."

He walked off and looked back as he saw Gaby raise her hands as if to say 'what the hell's he talking about' as she headed to the bar.

Joe thought that everything they had cemented over the last weeks had been destroyed in a couple of minutes. He headed to another bar and sat annoyed, angry, sad, and alone.

The next morning Joe had already packed one of his bags and was sitting downstairs as Gaby entered the room.

"Gaby... about last night."

"Yeah what the hell was wrong with you, you totally embarrassed me in front of my friends."

Joe found her comments astounding.

"I can't believe you're acting like this! You know how much she means to me and that if any of my friends needed me, I'd be there for them."

"Well run off and rescue her then."

Joe could see and smell Gaby was still very much hung-over from the previous night's session.

"I have to go now" he said, as he picked up his bag and headed to the door

"Yeah, whatever" he heard over his shoulder.

'What is her problem?' he thought as he headed down the street towards the station.

Joe also knew that he only had a week before he had to start work as a security officer, but work was not on the top of his priority list at the moment; Julia was.

He knew the journey well from London by now, and in an odd way it was strange going back as a civvie to where he had left as a soldier.

Joe arrived at the station and it was an odd five minute walk through the streets once again. The streets he knew so well, but this time it felt different. He entered the door to the Arms and as usual, Steve was leaning at the end of the bar reading his daily newspaper.

Steve left the bar and approached Joe and gave him a hug, which took him by surprise, but at the same time, he liked the idea of having a civilian friend.

As instructed, Joe dumped his bags in the spare room above the pub and headed back to the bar. Steve, being the ultimate host met him with his usual glass of wine and moved him towards his favourite table. In many ways Joe liked someone knowing what he wanted, but on the other hand, he hated the thought of being so predictable.

"Joe, I know how much Julia means to you. It didn't help that her old man came in one evening and saw her serving someone, and didn't like the way she smiled at him. It was totally innocent; he was in his late 50's and a regular."

"He didn't say anything at the time, but when she got home, that's when she said she had enjoyed the night out with us all. He then started laying into her physically." Joe could feel himself getting angry as Steve carried on.

"She called me the next day when he had gone to work. Maureen and I went around there and she was a complete mess." Steve went on to say that she had suffered a black eye and bruised ribs.

"We took her to the local hospital and sat with her all day until Mike came home. He went ballistic that we were there and that she had told anyone." Steve continued to explain that the Police were called after he threatened them, but typically Julia didn't want to press charges.

Before they left, Julia had told them she wished Joe was still around. Joe was fuming and trying to keep his cool, but so desperately wanted to go around there and beat the crap out of him. His head however was telling him to cool down and try to contact her. Steve agreed to call her the next day and tell her Joe was here.

For the rest of the evening, Joe sat by the bay window and drank more wine than he should have. He was still really annoyed at what had happened, but more so because he couldn't do anything; he felt helpless.

Joe woke feeling like crap. *'Why do I do this to myself?'* he questioned after all the wine he had consumed.

Maureen had heard Joe rising and put on a full fried breakfast and the smell wafted up the stairs to the room where he was stirring.

After the much welcomed meal, it was agreed that Maureen would call Julia after 10am when Mike had gone to work. It was the longest wait Joe had ever encountered.

After making the call, Steve placed down the receiver.

"OK, Joe. Maureen will go and pick her up and bring her here but she is feeling terrible, not just how she looks but about what happened."

"Thank you both so much."

Joe was on tenterhooks and as Maureen entered the private entrance at the back of the Arms, Joe stood up and waited to greet Julia. She entered the kitchen and Joe was shocked at how frail she looked. He went towards her.

"Please don't" she said.

Joe was devastated, he just wanted to hug her and to tell her everything would be alright. He stepped back and leaned against the sink.

"I am really sorry, Julia."

"What are you sorry for? It's not as though you did this."

"Can I do anything?"

"There isn't anything anyone can do."

Joe felt useless again, with all of his training and experiences, he really felt lost, let alone unwanted.

Julia explained what had happened and Joe felt his stomach turning as he heard about the pathetic, unprovoked attack inflicted upon her by Mike, the person who apparently loves her!

"Come away with me?" Joe asked without thinking the offer through.

He had nowhere to take her, but would have done anything to protect her from having to go through the same abuse again.

"I can't Joe. He needs me."

"Needs you? He beat the crap out of you."

Steve who had deliberately remained silent throughout piped up. "Joe, I know you want to do the best thing here, but Julia has to do what she thinks is right."

"Right, have him charged. Get out before it goes to the next level. Please leave him, baby."

"It's more complicated than that Joe."

Joe knew at this point that he was not going to change her mind. He had seen if before on active service in Northern Ireland, and even in his own regiment. He knew no matter what he had to say or offer, Julia would go back to the security of her husband.

He felt sad, sad for her, sad for the future and what she would have to endure.

"Julia, I am always here for you. You name it, it's yours" he said in a last desperate attempt to try to convince her she needed to leave him. "I know you are" she said as she continued looking at the ground, just as she had done since walking in.

Joe felt a strong urge to ask her to go with him right now, but where could they go? He couldn't really take her back to his sisters, and he had only been invited at Steve and Maureen's for the short term. He had nothing to offer Julia. No security, only a future.

He knew his words would fall on deaf ears, but he needed to try again.

"Baby, please listen to me. I am no expert, no shrink, but all I can tell you is that these things tend to escalate, and considering he has done this to you, what will he do next?" he asked.

"There is nothing I can do. He won't let me go."

"He says he loves me and it's me that makes him mad. It must be me that is in the wrong."

Joe wanted to erupt and carried on with gritted teeth watching his love cry.

"What! You know it's not you. It's him. It's all about him. It's his reverse psychology to control you. It obviously works."

It was the first time she had raised her head. "He loves me."

Joe felt real pain at that point and he knew that deep inside of Julia, she knew that was not true.

How could someone love someone and treat them in the way that he had, but he had seen the Stockholm syndrome situation before.

"I can't help you baby. I want to, but you really don't want to change what you have, and although, in an odd way I understand why, it can only be you that decides you want to change."

"I want you so much Julia, more than you will know, but I know you have security with Mike that I can't offer you. If you ever need anything, just call me. If not me, Steve or Maureen and I will keep in touch with them, but please know I love you. I will always be there for you."

Joe couldn't help but remember one of his own sayings he had used in various training sessions with new recruits relating to why people didn't want to, or couldn't, change; *In the beginning you hate it, then you realise it's easier to conform, and then you can't do without it. Welcome to the Army ladies and gents, this is your chosen life now.*' Those words were used before to sum up the institution of the military, but they are also true for many people that have, or are living in, a governed form. The military, prison, mental facilities or dictatorial relationships, it didn't matter which one you were in, they're all the same with the same approaches, pressures, risks, and controls.

"I had better go now" Julia said as she stood.

Maureen went to get the car and Joe stood and put his arm slightly forward really wanting her to hug him one last time. Julia looked at him with tears flowing from her eyes and placed her hand around his finger. Squeezing it tight, Joe could feel all of her love and emotions flowing through her and into him from that single touch. It said everything to him. She loved him and she knew he loved her.

"I am so, so sorry Joe" and with her parting words, she turned and left the room.

Joe sat with a heavy heart as his mind and body started juggling every emotion that he had ever experienced. He and Julia had known from the moment they had first looked into each other's eyes that they wanted each other and that they had something between them that few people rarely experience. Joe knew secretly that he loved her from the beginning, and he would do anything for her, yet he felt helpless and lost without her now, but in an odd way, he also understood what she needed to do and why.

"Come on Joe, I'll pour you a stiff drink."

They went through to the bar, and although it was still closed, Joe now saw the pub in a different light. It felt empty, as if it had lost its soul.

Joe sat looking out of the window with a glass in his hand for the remainder of the day. He closed his eyes and remembered her short breaks, and wanted to turn back the hands of time. *"Maybe I could have done something different. Maybe I could have stayed in the Army, would that have given her the security she needed?"* Joe questioned everything he had done, or should have done. He also blamed himself for what had happened to Julia and the loss of a woman's true love. He wanted to cry for the first time in his life with real pain in his heart. He felt sad and alone. Alone like only a person in love that has lost someone can feel. As strangers wandered past the window oblivious to this heartache he wondered how many others there were in a similar situation, simply living, to what appeared to others, a normal existence. He looked at every face, every corner, every passing car and every window wanting to see her beautiful face once more; she wasn't there.

He remembered her words when he had first told her that he loved her. Her response was ingrained on his brain; *"My gorgeous boy, I love you with my life, but my life is not my own to give."*

He should have known then where this would lead. Maybe he should have walked away, but he couldn't. He was pulled towards her; to the pain he now felt.

Joe was woken by Maureen.

"Joe, are you OK?" she enquired as he had fallen asleep in his chair at the table.

"I am sorry, I was shattered."

He noticed it was late afternoon as the sun had become lower in the sky, casting shadows across the grassed area opposite.

Maureen sat down and went on to explain that Julia had become distraught on her way back home, she had told Maureen that she loved him and she wished she had been brave enough to leave Mike, but she couldn't. There were too many ties and she wanted to apologise to him for that.

Maureen took Joe's hand and placed something in it and then closed his fingers around it.

"She wanted you to have this, and said that you will know what it means." Maureen left and headed back to the bar.

Joe immediately recognised the feel of the item in his closed hand. He smiled to himself as he began to open it to find she had given him an old coin that he knew had belonged to her father. A coin she had always kept in her purse. It was an Old English Penny struck and released in 1970; the year she was born.

Joe sat clutching the coin tightly closing his eyes and seeing Julia's soft, beautiful face. A tear ran down his cheek, and although he was so happy to have something of hers, he also felt guilty about taking something away from her that he knew she treasured and which had gave her comfort when she felt down.

THE ARREST

J oe needed to get away from people for a while and went for a walk along the High Street towards the castle and eventually found a bench opposite the chapel.

His thoughts were mixed, as were his emotions and he felt alone again, not just from being apart from Julia, he felt that most of the time, but his sister and his ex-colleagues too, despite being someone that had always preferred being on his own. He now felt the desperate need to be with Julia.

After some time of sitting watching the crowds pass by, he knew that he needed something to take his mind off of all the crap he was going through. He flicked through his contacts on his phone and found the number for George. He could do with someone who had always made him laugh and someone he had known for years.

George had always been a good friend and he felt guilty for not having contacted him since leaving.

"Hi George, its Joe."

"Good God man, I thought you had fallen off of the face of the earth."

Despite the offer of being invited back to the mess for a few drinks, Joe declined. He couldn't go back, not just yet, so they agreed to meet in a very modern and lively wine bar.

George entered and immediately headed over to Joe sitting at the bar with his back towards the door, and grabbed his arm.

"Your back's to the room Joe, you're losing your touch" he said as he laughed and gave Joe a bear hug.

"Bloody good to see you mate" Joe said.

"So what's been happening?" George enquired.

As they shared a bottle of wine, Joe told George everything that had been going on, from moving in with Gaby to the domestic situation with Julia.

George was a sensible person who thought about a reply, often at great length to the annoyance of others around him before commenting on most things.

"Hmm, Not a good position to be in for either of you."

"Is there anything I can do?"

"Not really my friend, just needed to sound off really."

"Sounds like you need a really good night out." As usual, George was right.

Joe called Steve and explained that he had met up with an old friend and that he may be late coming back. Steve told Joe where he would leave a key for him, but asked him to be quiet upon his return, and agreed it was a good idea to take his mind off Julia for a short time. Neither George nor Joe was fond of large groups or rowdy people.

On their odd night out or trip away, they tended to find a quiet bar and deposit themselves in a corner, and spend most of the time people watching and discussing everything but nothing.

The Fire Pit offered them what they needed. It was off one of the many cobbled side streets of the town and located in the basement of an old office block. It was a small, friendly and never packed sort of a bar, where the wine was exceptional and not the cheap sort found in a pub, but Joe was always grateful for the free glasses of wine he had received in the Arms.

George was a wine-lover too and they often had attended the mess's wine tasting evenings together. George had also accompanied Joe on various trips to see his friends, Simon and Jane. They were farmers in

Nottinghamshire who certainly knew how to entertain and who were seriously wonderful people. It wasn't until now that Joe thought what a great friend George was. It's funny how certain things happen in your life and how true friends stand up and be counted in times of need.

"Right Joe, how can we get you out of this spot you're in?"

"God knows."

"Have you thought about joining back up, you know you're still within the time limit?"

"I can't, for my own pride. It's not an option for me."

They discussed every available alternative from the most obvious and sensible ones, to the too-many-glasses-of-wine-later ridiculous and illegal ones.

At least they were laughing. Something Joe had not done in a long time.

Joe had always enjoyed George's company since their first meeting on a course so many years ago, and although they both served in different companies, they had always managed to catch up regularly. George worked in Support Company and their interaction on an official capacity was Joe coming to the stores.

George was not just a good guy, but one to be friends with, especially if you needed something. The mess bar was a good way to pay George back for the free kit he had accumulated over the years. More importantly, George was a genuine and great person to be around, both in and out of work.

After their third bottle, they headed back along the cobbled streets towards the barracks and the pub. As they turned onto the High Street, George suddenly shouted.

"Hey, get off him" as he ran towards a group of youths kicking ten bells out of someone laying on the floor.

Joe was impressed with George's response considering the amount of wine they had consumed and he ran in the same direction, but not quite at the same speed.

As he arrived the group had dispersed and George was holding a young boy in his arms. He had been severely beaten with various cuts around his face and head, as well as some serious swelling.

"Call an ambulance" George demanded.

As Joe was making the call, the boy lashed out at George and punched him in the face causing blood to spurt from George's nose.

"What the fuck!" George called out in shock at being attacked for trying to help.

Joe stopped talking to the operator and grabbed the boy's arm. "What are you doing? We're here to help."

The young boy continued to struggle but was well restrained.

"You need to keep still and listen to me" George repeatedly said.

The sirens of the emergency services could be heard getting nearer, and eventually arrived, but instead of the expected ambulance technicians, both George and Joe were dragged off of the youth by various police officers shouting at them together.

"Get on the floor, get on the floor. Face down, get on the floor" was all that could be heard.

They were both placed face down by three police officers each. Joe could feel handcuffs being placed tightly around his wrists as he tried to explain that they were helping the boy, but the voices of the police officers continued to drown out his own.

They were shoved in the back of a van despite their various pleas to be heard.

"What happened there?" George asked in disbelief.

"Bloody coppers think we attacked him, I think."

"They can't be serious?"

"I think they can and are. Why else would we be sitting in the back of a police van?"

The back doors to the van were opened by an authoritative-looking Police Officer.

"I am arresting you for assault. You do not have to say anything but it may harm your defence if you do not mention, when questioned something which you later rely on in court. Anything you do say may be used in evidence." Before they could say anything, the door of the van slammed shut again. Joe looked at George in surprise.

"I can't believe this."

The front doors of the van opened and closed and the vehicle moved off, it eventually swerved and came to a sudden stop forcing the occupants to slam against the internal cage. The doors were again forcibly opened and the two handcuffed prisoners were dragged out and escorted through a solid, steel door at the rear of a building.

"Stand there" one of the officers said.

They were both placed in front of a large, grubby looking desk from behind which various police and civilian staff were pottering around.

"Right" the desk Sergeant said, as the accompanying Police Officer with Joe pulled him forward.

"What we got?" he continued.

"Assault Sarg, in Downing Lane. These two hard nuts attacked a young boy who is currently receiving medical treatment in St Peters."

All the remaining details were taken and, after asking Joe his name and other personal details, it was explained what his legal rights were. The next process was to search them in which all of his personal belongings were taken from him, including Julia's penny and the embarrassing process of taking his DNA and fingerprints was carried out.

It was further explained to him that he was going to be placed in a cell, and the fact that he had refused legal representation meant that he would be in there all night. He was asked if he wanted to say anything and got the feeling no one was listening anyway, but thought it was worth the try.

"Bloody right I do!"

"If you swear again, Sir, I will have you arrested for a breach of the peace, understand?" the Sergeant snapped.

"We were passers-by helping the boy not assaulting him and we're dragged off like animals to be arrested. This is totally wrong."

"Hmm, I can also smell that you have been drinking. Typical" the Sergeant continued with a nonchalant attitude.

"It's not illegal to drink."

"But it is to assault someone. You squaddies are all the same."

'What's the point of arguing?' he thought.

They were both led away into separate small, tiled cells with a toilet in the corner and a concrete bed with a dirty and distorted mattress, that looked as though it had been used as a punch bag by the cell's previous occupants. The door slammed behind him.

'How the hell did all this happen?' he thought.

He was annoyed at the situation and more so the response of the police. He thought of George and wondered if he was alright and felt the same way.

The small hatch in the door noisily opened. "Hey, you alright in there?"

"I am, thank you, apart from being..." the hatch slammed closed, cutting Joe short from his protest of innocence.

"Great customer care" Joe said loudly.

He had never really had much time for the police when serving, as they had often hampered their exercises in the UK by pulling them over to warn them of the dangers of driving with heavy loads, checking their load straps, or they had not given them assistance when picking up soldiers absent without leave from various locations throughout the UK.

It had never been a good relationship between the two services, with the police thinking they place themselves in danger every day. They should try a spell on the ground of an operational tour when you really do place yourself at risk, every second of every minute. Every day, with no days off or a social structure built around you. They have no idea.

The hatch and noise game went on all night as if to keep those inside awake.

The next morning the cell door opened and a cup of coffee was thrust at him with little or no acceptance of his being there.

"Could I ask.." he started to say as the door hatch was slammed shut again.

'Idiots' he thought.

He looked around the cell and could see a path of worn tiles on the floor. He could see thump marks on the cell door, all a pattern of aggression from the cell's previous occupants but that was hardly surprising the way he was being treated. He sat there thinking that George and he did not belong here. They had done nothing wrong, yet these idiots had not bothered to ask them their version of events at the scene of that attack.

Eventually the cell door was opened and a couple of plain-clothed idiots walked in.

"Joe Forrester?"

"Yes that's me."

"Come with us please."

Joe was led to a small interview room.

The room was as shabby as the remainder of the station, with an array of dirt marks on the walls and floor as well as scratched markings on the furniture. 'Nice' he thought.

As he went to sit down he noticed that the chairs and table were screwed to the floor. A female entered the room and played around with the double tape deck.

"Mr. Forrester, may I remind you that you are still under caution" she said as the caution was repeated.

"I am Detective Stone and this is Detective Gunn. We are here to ask you questions about the attack on a youth last evening."

"Good, about bloody time. I have been shoved in a cell, treated like crap and all I did was to help someone that had been beaten half to death. Oh, and then met with an arrogant fuck-head of a Sergeant on the desk!"

"Sir, may we ask you to calm down."

"Why should I? You idiots have no idea how to deal with situations. You deal with drunks and thugs, but you treat those that help like criminals, it's pathetic."

The interview carried on bouncing back and forth and not really going anywhere fast.

After 2 hours, the leading detective piped up.

"Mr. Forrester, we are satisfied that you were not involved in the attack of the young male last evening. You are free to go." The tape was switched off.

"Gee, fucking thank you."

He was fuming inside as he was escorted back to the desk where he had been booked in to have a lecture on his rights, and given his personal belongings back before being escorted out of the station.

Joe started walking and wondered how George was. He was also really annoyed and angry at the way they had both been treated.

Joe made his way back to the pub and continually tried calling George with no success. He headed around the back door and looked for the key Steve had left, found it under the large plant pot and went to his room.

There was a knock at the door and Joe looked at his watch. It was 1pm.

"Are you there Joe?"

"I am Maureen, will be with you in a minute."

Joe wandered downstairs and entered the kitchen. Maureen was in the room starting the lunchtime food.

"It was obviously a good night out" Maureen stated.

"The opposite, it was crap" he said as he explained the sequence of events and how he had been treated.

Maureen was shocked.

"That is so bang out of order."

The discussion carried on as Maureen cooked. Whilst listening to her, Joe tried calling George a few times to make sure he was OK, and eventually got through. Not surprisingly, it transpired that he had also been released without charge. They agreed to meet up later that day.

It was 7pm when George entered the pub. Joe bought him a glass of wine.

"You're only allowed to have this if you don't run off to help anyone tonight" he said jokingly.

They sat and discussed the previous evening's events and their experience with the police and their pathetic levels of hospitality. George explained that he had to report to the Regimental Sergeant Major to answer for the arrests and how he had hit the roof. He went on to say that the 'boss' was going to formally complain to the police about how they had been treated. He had also mentioned that Joe should come and visit them in the mess.

"I can't go back there George."

Joe went on to explain that he didn't want to have to look back in his life, only forward, especially after losing Julia. George understood and explained that both he and his wife, Ann, would always be there for Joe. They spent the early evening chatting about old times and Joe's limited future plans. George left with a heavy heart as he felt for Joe and his situation, and he was concerned about his future. George had his career, but all Joe had was his sister now. They both agreed to stay in touch.

It was an early night for Joe and as he lay on the bed before he fell asleep, he couldn't help but think how crap life must be at times for Julia, and how he had lost her, as well as how much he missed her plus the guilt of his dead friends and his latest arrest. In one way he wished he had died instead of the three friends back in theatre; he felt low again.

Joe woke early and began thinking about the last few days again. He realised how much he needed to get back to Gaby's, away from Windsor and the associated memories. At least his sister offered him security, friendship and, at times, understanding. He needed that especially after what he had just experienced.

It was agreed that he was to head back that same day. Joe knew he had to confront her with the way he had left, but also wished she could understand his feelings. Unless you had travelled along that long and unchartered path, you couldn't understand it, nobody could.

By the time Joe arrived back home Gaby had gone to work. He let himself in and started to unpack his bag. When she arrived home late afternoon, Joe was already on his third glass of wine he had bought on his way back.

"Hi Joe."

"Hi you, how have you been?"

"Oh you know, getting by."

"I need to talk to you about my leaving."

They talked about Julia and her issues and again Gaby seemed nonplussed about the whole thing.

"OK what's your issue?" Joe asked.

Gaby went on to explain that she had previously had an affair with a married guy whose wife found out and went ape, so she understood what it felt like being on the receiving end of the anger.

Joe was again shocked at his sister's lifestyle. She had inflicted violence on her partner and then had an affair with a married man! The discussion carried on and eventually filtered out after getting nowhere quick.

"Goodnight" Gaby said as she wandered off to bed feeling hurt. "Night" he said, feeling the same.

Their relationship wouldn't allow either of them to back down or to admit defeat, and the evening's conversation had been full of defence for their own actions. Neither of them could see that they were talking to themselves rather than to each other.

The following few days were fraught with tension. They both pussy-footed around each other, but eventually, after a week, life seemed to get back to normal and the peace offering came from Gaby.

"Joe, I'm heading into town later with the guys from work, fancy joining us?"

"As long as you don't try to set me up again."

It was agreed that they would meet at 7pm in the usual wine bar near Gaby's work.

As usual, Gaby and her work colleagues were late, and as Joe sat in the corner drinking his glass of wine he wondered what the future would bring. It certainly wasn't a good start to his civilian life so far.

He had already decided he wasn't going to take the position he had secured as a security officer, especially after the run in with the police. *'After all, weren't jobs-worth security people wannabe police officers anyway?'* he thought.

He had only taken the course and vacancy as a temporary job until something better came along. He had always been a saver and had enough finances to see him through for some time, and although he had not told Gaby, he would have to soon as she would start asking questions. He would choose his time carefully to tell her depending on her mood.

Joe recognised the rowdy crowd as they entered the bar. "Hey, Bro!" Gaby shouted across the floor.

'Oh God, she's pissed again' he thought.

"Hi Gaby, you OK?"

The party of seven grabbed chairs from various tables and scattered themselves around Joe, which was their normal routine as they all started to talk loudly to each other.

"Here we go again" he said softly to himself.

The group consisted of a mixed bag of females, and they all seemed to enjoy their regular social gatherings, but he knew he didn't fit in. Not just with the group, but surrounded by others that appeared to have little, or no, personal scruples, and he was only there to be at his sister's beck and call to ferry drinks back and forth from the bar. A personal cross he had to carry for sharing her home.

Over the next couple of hours, Joe felt more uncomfortable and as Gaby and the rest were busy getting hammered, they didn't notice him moving to sit at the end of the bar, at least there no one ever stood to get served.

"What can I get you?" the barman asked.

"Large, white wine please."

As the glass was passed over to him, the barman tried to break into conversation.

"You OK, you seem a bit down for someone surrounded by loads of lovely woman all night?"

"Trust me, it's not all that!"

The young and smart barman felt the tension and left Joe to sulk over his wine.

Eventually Gaby came staggering across and asked Joe if he was ready to go. They made their way outside and took one of the many cabs waiting in the taxi rank.

On the way back Joe tried talking to his sister, but she started nodding off and falling asleep on his shoulder. The cab pulled up and, as usual, Joe paid and they entered the house with Joe supporting a rather unsteady sister.

He really wanted to talk to her. He was bored. He hated her usual nights out but felt as though he should go, he felt trapped in the house and its surroundings. He knew it was a waste of time that evening even trying again to chat. Probably anytime in reality, but he needed to tell her and he had to tell her soon.

GOING IT ALONE

The next morning Joe rose early and had breakfast on the go when Gaby wandered into the kitchen. There was a nod of a welcome from Gaby, her usual physical acknowledgement after one of her nights out.

"Gaby, I really need to chat to you" he said.

"God! Not now Joe."

"I feel trapped and bored. I need to do something with my life."

"Well you shouldn't have left the Army then, should you?"

"That's unfair."

The conversation started to become more aggressive.

"Joe, if you don't like it here then just leave!"

"I didn't say that. I'm not sure what I want. I was meant to start the security job but after the way I was treated by the police, I really don't want to become an arrogant jobs-worth."

"Your money can't last forever, and this is what real people do."

Joe felt hurt. *'Real people'* God, she had no idea of what was happening in the real world where *'real people'* fought for their lives on a daily basis. He continued to sit through further unwanted life pointers and eventually he grabbed his coat and headed out, not knowing where to go, but needing some space.

Despite being a loner, Joe felt alone as he wandered the streets. He didn't really know anyone here. He didn't want to call anyone due to the potential embarrassment of his situation, especially as he now had no job to go to.

He missed talking to someone like George who knew what he had experienced or felt, nor did he feel comfortable or wanted anymore within Gaby's home. He felt as though he would become a house slave to her, held to ransom despite it being his sister; he wasn't built for that way of life. This feeling was to continue for a number of weeks.

Joe wandered around until finding a cafe that was open. He sat there sipping his coffee and finishing his cooked breakfast looking around at his fellow, temporary residents. *'I am not one of these'* he thought. *'I don't belong here.'*

Still wandering around, Joe checked his watch and decided it was time for a much-needed drink to help him think. He headed to a nearby public house. He sat there drinking alone, people watching, one of his favorite pastimes.

He looked at the old men, the state scroungers and the sad, lonely people, wanting to either feel needed, or not caring about what people thought. Joe saw his life in civvie street ahead of him and didn't like what he saw. It made him angry, trapped and he drank more than he should have, which was becoming more and more of a frequent event. Joe eventually made his way back to Gaby's to find the house empty.

He opened another bottle of wine and sat at the kitchen table reflecting on his previous eating and drinking partners he found himself with early that day.

Gaby eventually came in, and although slightly frosty, took a glass of wine and headed off to have a soak in the bath. Joe almost felt robbed of his wine but he didn't say anything, after all he was a guest there, albeit a paying one.

The next couple of weeks remained the same daily process of Joe heading to local bars, with the conversations between him and Gaby becoming increasingly delicate, especially after one of Gaby's nights out.

With the tension, alcohol and Joe's longing for freedom, it wasn't long before the arguments started to increase and Joe started spending more time away from the house, especially as he couldn't help recalling his sister's aggressive past.

On one of the occasions that an argument took place about something or nothing, Gaby had stood up and started shouting and pointing. Joe had left the room before he felt the need to restrain her. It was when he was sitting in his room that he started to check what kit he had and what he would need to get away. He decided, just in case, to keep one bag packed with the essentials. It was what he was used to, planning for any eventuality. Luckily, knowing George, he had been able to keep the kit he wanted to within reason.

The bag was packed and a mental list made, but he made sure Julia's coin was on him at all times.

Sleeping bag

Bivvy bag

Washing and shaving kit

Spare clothes and underwear

Swiss Army knife

Para-cord

Duct tape

Dry rations

Regimental hip flask

Phone charger

Notepad and pen

Small bag of washing powder

The bag was shoved under the bed and he sat there thinking about the remainder of the items he could have packed, or maybe should pack. He could ask Steve to store the remainder of his stuff if needed, but then he and Maureen had done so much for him already.

In Gaby's absence one day, Joe checked out the attic. It was an empty, small and confined space, smaller than it should have been for the size of house, which no one had been in for years, including Gaby, that was obvious by the presence of spider webs and squeaking hinges of the ladder. The plan was hatched. Next time he had had enough, he would just leave.

That was to be much quicker than he had anticipated.

The following morning, Joe rose late to avoid Gaby and listened to her leaving the house. He didn't know if she had deliberately slammed the front door harder than she normally did, or it was his paranoia with the situation.

He took his time getting ready and having breakfast, but he eventually took his daily stroll down 'loserville' street as he had re-named the High Street, and headed into a small old-looking pub.

He had tried going into different public houses so as not to become acquainted with any specific pub, or to become too familiar with the locals in order to avoid a conversation.

He had noticed the White Hart and had, for some strange reason, remembered the name being associated with the support for King Richard II, but couldn't remember the exact historical attachment. He sniggered to himself as he thought that he had never bumped into anyone called Richard in any of the other same-named pubs.

The pub was quiet as the majority of them were just after midday. The interior had wood-panelled walls with soft, leather chairs scattered around the small lounge area.

"Morning Governor" the elderly gentleman said from behind the dimly lit bar.

After a small silence, Joe asked for his normal tipple of a large glass of wine. As he was waiting for it to be poured, and as Joe was taking in the smell of old spilt beer on carpets, the barman piped up again.

"Not seen you in here before. Live locally?"

Joe hated people fishing for information.

"No, only visiting."

"Anyone we might know?"

Apart from pulling the barman over the counter and telling him to shut up, there was little he could do to stop the barrage of questions. Joe had decided to lie from the outset and had told him he was from Kent. He was a Landscape gardener and was up here on business. It seemed a plausible story; or so he thought!

"How would I sort out an old tree stump I have in the garden?" the barman asked.

Joe wasn't sure if this was a test question or the barman really did have one and he was taken aback a little, but tried to reply.

"Depends on what tree it is." Thankfully one of the courses he had taken many years back was that of an Assault Pioneer which involved cutting and blowing up trees amongst other things.

The barman's reply was cut short as another customer entered.

"Oh thanks for that, I'll have to check that out" he said disinterested as he headed to serve someone that obviously wanted to chat in more detail than he did.

Joe sat there for some time, and although each drink ordered was followed by another round of questions, Joe got shorter and shorter with his responses. The unspoken and eventually agreed silence allowed Joe to feel more comfortable with his surroundings, and for a change, he felt fairly comfortable.

He sat there at ease which was made easier with the glasses of wine he was consuming, and not really thinking about anything important. He did however wonder how Julia was, as he did all of the time and if Mike had been any better to her, he really hoped so. Julia was far too good for him, but he had controlled her for so long, she didn't really know how to change the circumstances. He missed her terribly.

As Joe left the bar, he found the early evening had a bit of a chill, and turned up his collar as he slowly headed back towards Gaby's. As he was about to leave the high Street, he decided to have one more drink in small bistro bar. He had been in there a couple of times, and had liked the atmosphere compared to the majority of places he visited. He sat at the bar, which for Joe in the local area was unusual as it was far too near people that liked to chat. The bar was well lit and had a young feel to it, and the people working were always young and non- intrusive unlike the other bars and pubs. He sat there relaxed, the most he had in a number of weeks. He didn't want to go back home, but he couldn't stay out either. He ordered another drink and some tapas.

Joe eventually went back to the house feeling good. He entered the house and as usual went to the kitchen to grab another glass of wine. As he started to open the door, he heard someone scrambling around, and being suspicious he burst in only to find his sister half-dressed pulling her clothes together and a young guy standing there doing the same.

"God, so sorry Gaby" he said in embarrassment as he turned and left the room.

"Who the fuck is that?" the unknown male guest asked.

"That's just my bloody brother!"

He heard some loud voices from his room and then the front door slam again.

"Joe, I want you down here right now!" His sister shouted.

'Here we go' he thought to himself.

As Joe entered the living room, he tried to apologise.

"Gaby, I am so..." he was cut short.

"I want you out Joe, right now. I've had enough of us pussy footing around, and I can't feel comfortable in my own home anymore."

Joe was surprised at her aggression and although he tried to apologise again, he was met with resistance to any balanced discussion. Joe left the room and headed back up to his room. He knew he had to get out right there and then.

He slid back the hatch to the attic and threw in his non-essential luggage, grabbed his emergency bag and headed out of the door without saying anything else to his half-cut sister. He had deliberately kept the front door key, and knew he could come back at any time Gaby to get his gear as he knew she wasn't sensible enough to have the locks changed.

It was a cold night and Joe had decided to try to head to somewhere and to someone he knew well, back to Windsor, plus it was the only place he wanted to be.

The few minutes' walk to the station gave him time to calm down and regroup his thoughts. The tube ride into central London was also uneventful and after arriving at Paddington station, he checked the latest train times for the remainder of his journey.

"Bloody typical!" he said out loud as he slammed his hand on the timetable on the wall, he had missed the last train.

Having been in similar situations in the past, he wasn't that worried and he found a concealed corner and commenced to try to get his head down for the night in the usual squaddie style of coat over the head and bag under the legs.

The night was cold, but Joe had been through worse. As he sat there listening to the night sounds of the station from the small driven cleaning machine to shutters closing in the small retail outlets he realised that officially, he was now classed as homeless! Not a situation he had expected to find himself in.

He woke suddenly as he felt a prod in his legs, and quickly threw back the coat to find two British Transport Police Officers standing there.

"You can't sleep here son."

"Sorry I missed my last train and had nowhere to go."

They had heard it all before, and despite Joe's explanation and need to find somewhere to sleep, they escorted him from the station.

Joe was now stuffed for a place to sleep undercover, so he decided to head towards Waterloo where he could get a direct train rather than having to change from Paddington the following morning. The walk didn't bother him as he made his way towards the Thames. He could feel and smell the night air of the river and the city he knew so well.

He knew that by the arches by Waterloo station there was a soup wagon for the homeless. He had used it once before when stranded with a few friends on their way back to the Union Jack Club accommodation, a well used military hotel, and as long as he was officially classed as homeless, he may as well get some free soup and a bread roll.

The queue at the wagon was full of a variety of people from true down and out homeless people, to city workers hoping for a free meal, and everyone you can imagine in between.

He felt as though he was taking away from the needy, those truly hungry so he turned and walked away.

The station was closed, and he again walked around trying to find another safe sleeping location. The South Bank was the nearest place which he knew had many overhanging walkways, and he eventually found one which had been unofficially transformed into a skateboard park.

He noticed two others already occupying the furthest corner and he moved to one of the small knee high walls and again assumed the position of rough sleeping he had so many times before in military vehicles or in forward operating bases. It allowed him a quick reaction to unwanted attention and to react to any potential incident, after all he was an experienced and hardened soldier.

He had little to fear from the streets of London as he took a swig of whisky from the hip flask before tucking it back into his bag.

The night was cold, especially through the concrete slabs underneath. At various times, he had thought about getting out his sleeping bag, but as normal, it was too much trouble in case he was moved on, or had to bug out again at short notice. He dozed off hiding from the world, as well as the weather.

The coat blocked some of the kick to the side of his head, but it couldn't stop it from hitting the wall. The physical pain shot through him and he tried to pull back the coat and defend himself, but he was disoriented and he stumbled to his feet.

He tried to focus only to feel another blow to the face. He stumbled back and clenched his fist, he could hardly see, but the vision, despite being blurred could make out three figures, male and young, but the details were still obscure. He felt another shot of pain in his stomach and he fell to the ground. The next set of blows he didn't feel as the light faded away.

The pain started to escalate in Joe's body as he started to come around. He could see light through his eyelids, but he didn't know where he was or what had happened. The light started to get brighter and he could feel his body moving through no physical action of his own.

The voices were distant and he could see shadow type figures. It took a couple of minutes to come around.

"Come on wake up. Talk to me."

Joe really didn't know where he was or what was happening. Eventually, he started to feel some serious pain and the vision started to come back.

He had been sat up and had three people kneeling in front of him. He recognised the uniform of a paramedic and those of police around them. He was unable to speak to respond to their questions, but he knew his body had suffered some sort of trauma. He had experienced the same thing some years previous in Iraq where he had been knocked off of his feet in an explosion. The loss of hearing, the intense pain and the half conscious thoughts felt the same. *'Am I back there?'* he thought.

After what seemed like an eternity, he started to come around. He felt restrained as he became aware that he had been placed on a stretcher and he was in the back of an ambulance. He was also aware of a police officer sitting in the back.

"How are you feeling?" the young paramedic said.

"Like shit" Joe slowly replied.

"Do you know what happened?"

"I'm not sure, I think three men set about me" he replied as he started to recall the attack.

The police officer jumped in.

"Can you give me a description of any of them?"

"I didn't really see them."

"Typical, too pissed were we?"

"You fuck-head, what is wrong with you idiots?"

"Please leave the vehicle for a minute" the paramedic instructed the officer.

"OK, you have been beaten fairly badly, and have some facial, head and body cuts and bruises as well a suspected broken rib or two. Can you tell me your name?"

"It's Joe. Joe Forrester."

His details were taken, but he couldn't remember any contact details. "If you pass me my bag, I can get one for you."

"There are no belongings here with you" was the response, which he found hard to accept.

"I had a bag with me."

"It's not here now, and we have searched the area and couldn't find anything" she continued.

"Check my jeans pocket. Is there a coin in there?"

The paramedic checked and eventually found the coin that Julia had given him in the small hidden coin pocket.

"Thank God" he said to himself.

"We're going to take you to St Thomas's hospital for a check-up."

"No, I'm OK, really."

"I seriously think you should come along with us, you're in a bad way."

"No I'll be Ok."

After a few minutes, he was released out of their charge and he sat on the small wall next to where he had been sleeping. Although his head was throbbing, and his sides hurting with every breath, he knew he would be fine as he watched the ambulance and police car drive off.

"Hey buddy, you OK?" came a voice from the other corner.

"Yeah fucking great!"

The lone figure came over and told Joe that he had seen what had happened and that he had tried to tell the police but as he was homeless, he was told to get lost.

"Why the fuck didn't you step in?" Joe asked with anger in his voice. "Trust me, you learn to keep out of other people's business."

"I'm Caelan" he said as he extended his hand.

"Joe" he replied and shook his witness's hand.

"I take it you have nothing left now?"

"Only what I have in my pockets." He tapped to see what he had left.

Joe could feel his wallet as he had always kept it in his hidden 'poachers' pocket of his coat, as well as a small torch on a single key to Gaby's house he kept in the same pouch.

"Great personal belongings hey?" Joe said as he raised the old penny. "More than I had when I first hit the streets."

"Look, why don't you come with me and we'll try to sort something out?"

Joe had no choice only to follow this unknown homeless person or to just sit there.

Joe's life was about to change forever as he followed Caelan.

Joe was taken to an old boarded up archway where his new carer commenced to move a small part of the board to reveal a small hole which he was ushered to get into sharpish. After painfully struggling through, inside were a number of small makeshift cardboard huts with odd bits of plastic bags and sheets scattered around them which were just high enough to sit and sleep in. All of them were the length of an average person.

"It's not much, but its home and it's safe."

Joe was surprised at the mock living quarters and how dry it was. Caelan went on to explain that he was shown it by someone who later moved on and he *gave* him his spot for a swap of some food.

"Life's like that here on the streets, you don't get anything for nothing" he said as he tapped Joe's arm.

Joe was made welcomed by the other three occupants who were sitting around drinking cans of beer, and offered him a drink.

"No thanks."

They sat chatting for a while and Joe agreed to spend the night and assess his injuries the following morning. He was in pain with his head and ribs, but he knew it would subside. He was given some spare cardboard and shown how to use it and the newspapers to keep warm.

Joe lay there cold and feeling vulnerable as his body was still in shock. He couldn't believe how he had been taken by surprise let alone injured. He had failed! All these years of training, all those years spent roughing it around the world and he ends up on the streets of London! How could he now go back and face anyone in this state.

Caelan offered him a retreat for him to take a step back and regroup his thoughts. He was a mental and physical mess and needed to sort himself out.

Joe couldn't sleep, his mind kept on wandering all over the place. He thought of Julia and how she would disown him if she could see him now. He was used to feeling alone and sad, but this time, he also felt lost and for the first time in his civilian life, frightened!

He had money in the bank but that was it. Apart from the bags he shoved in Gaby's attic and Julia's penny, he had nothing else.

He felt too embarrassed to try to contact anyone and in an odd way, life on the streets offered only two things. The first was a struggling existence. The second was a strange sense of freedom.

Days turned into weeks living in the archway and Joe's physical injuries healed, but the mental ones remained which often led to sleepless nights and flash-backs of his traumatic experiences in the Army. Maybe this was penance for his three friends he felt he had killed.

He was careful not to tell anyone he had his wallet and access to money and rarely had to touch it. The pound as much as it seems important to most people, is not the currency of the street and certainly doesn't help you when you're sleeping rough.

Life on the street is a real struggle, much harder than anything Joe had experienced before. It is literally a struggle for survival not just with each other, but with the elements, the need to search for food and water, keeping clean and more noticeable than any of those, being an outcast from society.

Even muggings and beatings were common-place within the homeless community, let alone local gangs or pissed-up city workers having a go at them on a regular basis. These and more were all a part of daily life for the unfortunate street people, or to the general population, the invisible non-working gutter class.

No one liked being homeless, but for some it was better than being a part of a corrupt and aggressively competitive society. For others, they simply had nowhere to go either through their own choosing or through circumstance.

There was a mix of people from a variety of different backgrounds ranging from sex abuse victims to upper class rejects. Whatever their background, Joe was now one of them, with nowhere to go, and no one to care for apart from himself.

Caelan started showed him the ropes and the tips he had taught himself to get by. It is amazing how resourceful the homeless can be, and in many ways, Joe was experiencing what the average member of the public either turns a blind eye too, or mock. Although initially Joe was dubious about his street mentor, eventually they came to trust each other as the days and weeks went by.

Joe learned that Caelan was also an ex-serving soldier who had fallen on hard times after his tour of Iraq. He also had some psychological issues he didn't want to discuss with Joe, or anyone else, and he would often have nightmares or sometimes not sleep. Joe knew what he was going through but didn't say anything, no one ever did.

Everyone had their own story. Their own nightmares and their own fears, but no one cares on the streets. You're all in the same pile of crap with different views, resentments and issues.

Caelan was one of the lucky ones, and had been living on the streets for 2 years and had a good clean regime going, as much as one could on the streets. Using all the resources available from pub toilets for washing and shaving as well as taking the toilet rolls, through to entering hotels by the workman's entrances to use the showers, find food and get clean clothes from the laundry. He had also seen his fair share of those that did not or, could not, be as resourceful, or in some cases even be bothered.

It may be immoral or illegal but it was what was needed to get by and, after all, it was not as if they were harming any individual, and businesses could afford it, plus it was living on the basic survival needs that Maslow had so often referred to.

There was though an element of those sleeping rough that were violent. Those that did attack for money usually had to do so to fuel their habit of drink or drugs, and in some cases both. These are the ones you need to keep clear of as they will go to any lengths to get what they want, no matter what it was. Your arse or your shelter, it was all the same to them. They wanted it, they got it.

They chatted regularly about military life and what they had both once been a part of, the larger family in which they had no choice but to trust each other implicitly.

"Why do you hang around this part of London with so much trouble and agro, have you not thought of heading further out?" Joe asked.

"I feel like a modern day Dodger out of Oliver Twist. It's just a game of survival. It's a skill you have to get used to and it can pay its rewards depending on what you want."

"But what if there was somewhere else more safe and secure where we lived off of the land as well as the streets?"

"Where are you thinking?"

"God knows! Maybe we just walk out of town and see. Near where my sister lives there are green areas, let's give it a go? With our combined skills, surely we can't fail, or somewhere else like Highgate cemetery. I used to go there as a boy, that's pretty rundown and hardly anyone goes to some parts anymore."

The same conversation took place over a number of weeks, with planning from taking the first step to having new sleeping areas being made, and, as the struggle for daily existence continued, Caelan was warming to the idea, especially as they witnessed time and time again muggings, beatings, death, hunger and disease. Only those living rough can truly know how vicious the streets can be and what little help there is for those needing it so badly.

There is a street way of dealing with their own in need of help, and it's not as nice or as pleasant as one may like to know, or even think about. It really is a dog-eat-dog world in so many ways!

Joe had one more trick up his sleeve.

"Here I got you this today" Joe said as he handed Caelan a small bottle of whisky.

"Where the hell did you get this?"

"Don't worry, I didn't steal it!"

They sat and drank in their usual secure night-spot behind the billboard. Luckily the other occupants half the time looked as though they were already dead, not taking any interest in anyone or anything.

The deal was done! Caelan had finally given in.

"OK let's give it a go, but if it's not better in a couple of days, I'm coming back."

'Surely the grass had to be greener on the other side of London?' Joe thought.

The next morning their limited belongings were gathered. It was a waste of time even mentioning to the other billboard residents that they were heading off. They pulled the small board to one side for the last time and headed north from the city, passing by the Houses of Parliament and Regent's Park where they slept the first night in the open air.

They walked with a pace as if they had a mission to accomplish, or force marching again. Within two days they arrived at the entrance to the cemetery.

It was a grand building with a gated archway in the centre allowing tourists to gather, pay and enter. The ground-keeper's gate was already open and they entered without being seen past the parked cars.

Walking into certain parts of the centre of the cemetery is like walking into a secondary jungle. The headstones and tombs had given way to Mother Nature as the ivy, roots and vines over time had slowly crept across the landscape to form a canopy of natural camouflage. It was an eerie place but one that also had a natural beauty, as the sunlight shone through the gaps in the trees and ivy to make rippling patterns on the wet grass below.

The cemetery also had a calming effect, with little noise being heard from outside this hidden wonderland with its array of strange headstones ranging from angels to pianos. The smile and nod from Caelan confirmed it was a good choice. Could this be the safe haven they had hoped for?

THE PLOT

Walking through the tranquil pathways of the cemetery was a different world from the boarded archway they were used to, as they passed by so many potential places to stay. Places built into the hillside, but they eventually found what would be their new home, the circle of Lebanon in the west side of the cemetery.

As they walked around the circle there were tombs with large doors on either side, all with inscriptions of their deceased guests. Numerous doors were broken and it wasn't long before they came across one that could be accessed by crouching down.

Joe had his torch and could see that no one had been in these for decades. The entrance was covered with ivy and cobwebs, and once cleared, revealed a large stone room with a raised tomb on either side. The room reminded Joe of a crappy hotel room he had stayed in once with two beds and nothing else.

"It's perfect!" Caelan said.

They dumped the limited items they had brought with them and commenced cleaning their new living quarters of the leaves and cobwebs gathered over the years.

The flat-topped tombs made excellent beds once cardboard had been placed out, and the small hole at the end of the tomb would make an excellent ventilation shaft for a small fire. It didn't take long before they were settled in.

"Why the hell didn't I do this ages ago?" Caelan asked as he passed over the small and half empty bottle of whisky.

"Cheers!" Joe said as he swigged the bottle and had that after facial muscle-wrenching affect.

It was the first good night's sleep they had both had in a long time, more so for Caelan.

The sun was soon shinning and they emerged to greet the day, to explore their new home as well as to search for the basics needed to commence life in the new and isolated environment.

The lake in the cemetery was perfect for their water needs and, of course, it attracted a variety of wildlife. The next few days were spent collecting and scavenging all the items that could be of use, as well as setting traps and dodging the tourists who were allowed in for a one hour tour each day, wandering mostly around the east side of the cemetery. It is comical what people leave on graves that can be of use to the homeless.

Highgate Cemetery is now home to some famous people such as Karl Marx, Max Wall and Joe's favorite, Robert Grant VC. Grant won the highest gallantry award saving a comrade in the Indian mutiny in 1857 but later died of consumption and buried in plot number 15054. A pauper's grave not worthy of a war hero, but a new headstone was later placed on the plot by his family some years later.

Joe was to visit the grave regularly over his time there and think of his lost friends whom he had failed to keep safe.

No one ever came to the area of the circle and it was ideal for their needs. The skills learnt within the armed forces were certainly being tested, and Joe was chuffed he had completed both jungle training and survival courses over the years, as his knowledge certainly helped them live well over the following few weeks.

Their 'room' was also transformed into a safe and comfortable place to stay, and an old stone slab was found to be placed on the inside to block the hole of an evening from any unwanted animal or human visitors.

In the evenings when it was dry, they would often sit on top of the circle and watch the stars; it reminded them both of being out in the field back in the forces. It was on one of these occasions they discussed the numbers of ex-forces on the streets.

Caelan had come across so many, and again, they all have their own reasons for choosing such an existence. The majority however appeared like Caelan himself to have suffered from issues arising from their time in a conflict zone.

"It's a pity we couldn't bring a few of them here. It's safe, plus it's not as though we're short of space" Joe said.

"I'm not so sure. The more people, the more resources that are needed."

The same discussion would be repeated on various occasions, and the more they settled in to their new environment, the more they felt as though they had abandoned the larger, homeless community; the balance between their own security and wanting to help others always fell heavily on their own conscience.

Amongst those unfortunates living rough, there are some that eventually make it back into some form of society, others that pay the ultimate price through extreme conditions, drugs, alcohol or hunger and there are those rare individuals that learn to live reasonably well with limited resources. Joe and Caelan were in the latter group; they were the lucky ones, but they knew many who were not.

For Joe and Caelan, life was easy. No authority to tell them what to do, pleasing themselves with no responsibility to anyone or anything.

Joe still missed Julia and thought of her regularly with a passion, yet he knew deep inside that he couldn't get in touch; he would be too embarrassed. He often held the penny that she had given him in his hand and he would close his eyes to see her beautiful face. He may not be with her but she had, and always would have, a special place in his heart as he knew he did in hers.

When leaving the tomb one of them would always remain in the circle to ensure their 'room' would be safe from intrusion, and the well-practiced screeching noise of a fox was their warning that it was one of them that was approaching.

They had an agreed set of operating procedures including an emergency meeting location, in case they needed to quickly vacate the tomb for any reason and their limited personal belongings would never be in one position.

They would take it in turns to walk into the main shopping area to see what they could get for free. Joe would sometimes secretly head to the cash point and purchase items, such as clothes from a charity shop, pots and food and tell Caelan he had managed to get them from a skip or that he had sat and begged for a short time.

Caelan was always dubious how he seemed to be more successful than he was, but never complained as he benefitted from his 'scrounging' ability too.

They shared most things, life was good for them and the weather was holding out. They collected items from a variety of different sources to see them through the forthcoming winter, they both knew it was going to be hard and winter on the streets can be lethal as temperatures drop well below freezing, and no matter how much you try to keep warm, the cold is there waiting to claim its next victim.

Although there are limited charity hostels, they tended to be fully occupied, and usually with the first drunks to arrive as the night falls in. The majority of those sleeping rough, the really needy, don't bother going to them as it means mingling with others and being sociable. That is not a general trait of the homeless.

In the late evenings, Joe liked to walk the perimeter of the cemetery for exercise; to check on the pre-set traps and to ensure there were no signs of any other unwanted visitors. It was a good feeling creeping around the grounds and it reminded him of patrolling in the Army.

Putting all of his previously acquired military skills to the test, he once again began to move through the undergrowth silently, and with ease.

The evening and night wildlife was amazing and creatures such as badgers, foxes and muntjac deer roamed around freely; Joe felt at one with nature as he treated the area as his own personal English wildlife park where he and Caelan were the only visitors.

It was on one of his evening patrols that Joe noticed two cars parked near one of the small isolated entrances along one of the quiet lanes adjacent to the cemetery, and although the vehicle lights were out, Joe could make out two people standing leaning against the cemetery wall. Making his way silently towards them, he began to make out two middle-aged, white males with local accents. One was small with a bald head and the other was a fat guy with what looked like a pony-tail.

"So were in agreement then?" asked the small guy.

"Yeah can't wait to get the bastards. We just need to arrange the resources."

They continued chatting and agreed to meet next week at the same time and same isolated location. Joe watched the vehicles leave with their individual occupants.

As he wandered back to the circle he wondered what they were planning, and who were the 'bastards' they referred to.

He spent the remainder of the night laying there knowing something wasn't right. It wasn't until the next morning that he told Caelan what he had witnessed.

"Don't get involved, mate."

"Something isn't right. It's been playing on my mind."

"Seriously, leave it."

Joe knew he couldn't and as each day passed, he looked forward to their next meeting.

Every evening prior to their next meet Joe checked out the same spot he had first overheard the two men chatting, and commenced to make a hide near the railings in preparation.

As a previously trained military sniper and close observation operative, he was used to setting up locations near to a target and, more importantly, living silently until the right moment came along; no matter how long it took. All it required now was for his unknown planners to return as they had previously agreed.

The day finally arrived and although it seemed to drag by, the sun eventually began to set. Joe was already in the hide when he heard the first car arrive. It was a dark saloon and as it slowly pulled up to gates, he could see it was 'Mr. B,' as he had come to refer to the small bald guy.

He got out of the car and started playing with his mobile. After about 10 minutes it rang.

"Where are you?"

"What? Bloody hurry up, will you? Lots to talk about" he said as he cancelled the call.

Eventually another vehicle could be heard approaching again, as with the first it had no headlights on. It stopped next to Mr. B's car.

"About bloody time!" he said as Mr. F exited his dark large family style car.

"OK, I'm here now stop moaning."

"OK, finances secured. We have a team of 20 volunteers in all locations, but we now need to purchase the explosives." Joe wasn't expecting to hear that as a surprised look came on his face.

"OK, I'll leave the contact details in the usual place for someone who can assist you with that."

"We only have one chance to get this right and I don't want your guys backing out."

"OK, tomorrow night?"

"Cool, see you then."

Mr. B got in his car and drove off.

The remaining plotter stayed for a short time, pulled out a large map of the UK and made a call.

"Hey, who do we have in Liverpool, Glasgow, Windsor and Sheffield?"

"OK. Let's get some people we can trust and call me as soon as."

He cancelled the call and put the phone in his pocket before throwing the map in the passenger side of the car as he entered the driver's seat. He drove away from the area with the lights of his vehicle still turned off.

Joe waited for a short time before leaving the hide and headed straight back to the circle. Caelan was awake when Joe entered.

"Listen, I need to tell you something and you need to hear this."

He told him about the plot he had overheard, and how concerned he was witnessing the planning stage of an attack on the locations previously mentioned.

"Are you sure they didn't know you were there and were saying it for your benefit?"

"What! No chance. Come with me now."

Caelan was impressed with the hide and could see that it was within four feet of the location of the cars and planners. Caelan took his usual stance of not wanting to get involved.

"Listen Caelan. We need to report this to the police."

"Oh, yeah, two homeless guys living in a cemetery illegally, they're really going to listen to us!"

"We need to try."

"Why don't you find out more tomorrow night, if they turn up again, and we can take it from there?"

The plan was set and they headed back to the circle. Joe couldn't sleep and he lay there thinking about what he had heard. *'Shit!'* he thought to himself as he remembered they had mentioned Windsor as a potential target.

He would find out more tomorrow and, as well as telling the police, if needed he would phone Steve and George and tell them of the attacks. Joe couldn't sleep. He was eager to find out more, but wanted to get Caelan's help rather than having to go this alone.

As the sun was rising, Joe was already up having washed and shaved by the time Caelan showed his face. Joe had already been to one of the traps and had started cooking breakfast.

"Fish again I'm afraid. I was all out of bacon and eggs."

When living rough, you soon learnt to eat when you can, but it still doesn't stop you dreaming about luxuries. The small tin pot was also on the fire for boiling water for the tea, and they sat around the welcomed warmth from the fire. There was something about the smell of burning wood that Joe had always loved, as it reminded him of when he used to go camping on Dartmoor as a child with his cousins.

The day was uneventful as Caelan headed out for his usual foraging trip into town, whilst Joe stayed behind and double-checked the hide again before the cemetery keepers and the public arrived for their daily tour.

He sat around waiting for the day to end so he could get back to what had been playing on his mind.

Caelan returned back with his usual limited find but this time he had found some well-needed tarpaulin and plastic sheeting which would replace the leaking sheet used to cover up their hidden supplies in the undergrowth.

Joe was itching to get back to the hide, but Caelan wasn't interested in the obsession that seemed to have taken over his thoughts.

Joe was again settled into the hide and waited much longer than he had on the previous meeting nights, and eventually, as was now normal procedure for the planners, one turned up before the other each slowly creeping up the lane with no lights on their respective vehicles.

"We have secured the items" Mr. B said.

"Good. Now we just need to get the details of the contacts and we can agree the rest."

"Look on here."

He pulled out various maps.

"Changing the Guard in London and Windsor. The opening of the new museum in Sheffield, the return of HMS Brigadoon in Liverpool as well as the trade fair in Glasgow. Oh, and not forgetting the boat race in Brighton. We'll hit the lot of them on the same day and at the same time. The UK will come to a stand-still. It's then we put plan 'b' into operation and really screw them up!"

"Are we still sure we have not been compromised?"

"Be fucking serious, we're using the same trusted people as we have before. No one will have a clue. You wait and see."

"OK. Change phones tonight and be back here on Saturday."

It was obvious Mr. B was the operational liaison and Mr. F the fixer, the one with the contacts and financial support. They left as they had arrived.

Joe had to convince Caelan they should now do something. He was asleep when Joe entered the tomb.

"Hey, wake up."

"Oh, great it's Miss Marple."

Joe explained what he had overheard, and he could see Caelan slowly rising and listening intensely.

"Shit!"

"I'm heading to a police station to tell them."

"Good idea, do you need me to do anything?"

Joe was surprised as it was the first time he had volunteered his help or been even remotely interested.

"Check the hide daily to make sure it's not been tampered with in the morning and just wait here until I get back."

"Joe. What if they ask you how you know about this shit? We could get found here and thrown out."

"Leave that to me. We won't be compromised." He turned and exited the tomb in a hurry.

ALL ALONE

Joe had passed by a police station on his occasional trips into town, and headed straight there making sure he wasn't followed.

The station was a typical 70's style grey slab building and Joe entered the main glass entrance. He looked around to find the reception full of relatives trying to track down those that had been arrested the previous night, as well as drunks trying to string a few words together, let alone an understandable sentence.

Eventually using the supermarket style ticket machine, number 441 came up and Joe stepped forward to the civvie behind the desk who looked Joe up and down. Although he wasn't as bad as the majority of those sleeping rough, it was obvious he was homeless.

"Here we go" he said as Joe stepped forward.

"Want a bed for the night or a free meal do we?" the cocky middle-aged, self-important desk operative said.

"I need to speak with a police officer or the Counter Terrorist Unit urgently."

"Of course you do."

"Listen, you fuck-head, I want to report an attack that's being planned."

"Right, that's it. Get out" the desk officer stated as he rang a bell asking for assistance.

Joe stood there in disbelief at the lack of interest in what potentially could be a devastating and lethal attack on the general public and military.

Two uniformed officers came from a wooden side-door and grabbed Joe by the arm.

"Hey, what you doing?" he protested as they man-handled him to the door.

"I am being serious. I want to report a potential terrorist attack." At the main door they shoved him out and, as they turned away, he heard them mutter "Bloody homeless! They will try anything to get a free meal."

Joe was fuming and couldn't believe he had simply been fobbed off. He resentfully made his way back to the circle in disbelief of their arrogant attitude towards him. Not just a homeless person, but somebody with information that could hopefully save hundreds, if not thousands, of lives.

As he slowly wandered back, the situation reminded him of the 1970's bombing of a pub in Surrey. Prior to the explosion, one of the inmates from the local mental institution told the bar staff there was an unattended bag under one of the seats. They laughed at him, gave him a drink and ignored his repeated concerns; he was known as The Sheriff as he used to check the pub and the surrounding area on a daily basis. The Sheriff left shortly after warning the bar staff.

The bomb exploded some fifteen minutes later severely injuring 23. Joe didn't want any spilt blood on his hands. He needed to re-think his next move, and fast.

"I told you. They're not interested in anything we have to say."

"I can't just let it go, especially as they may target Windsor, my old regiment, my friends and more important, Julia."

"It's now out of your hands. At least here you're safe."

Joe couldn't sleep and stayed awake for the remainder of the night. Early the next morning, he headed into town, despite Caelan's warning to keep away and forget about the two unknown males. Joe had to try the police again.

He repeated the process of taking a ticket and waiting his turn, he noticed that it was a different operative behind the desk, which gave him a glimmer of hope that he would finally be listened to.

His turn eventually came again.

"I would like to speak to someone in charge as I have some information that may be of interest."

"OK. What's it about?"

"It's about a potential terrorist attack."

"Oh OK. You came in earlier didn't you?"

"Yes. Why?"

"Ok. Go on, off you go now, and stop spreading stupid rumors."

"I am sick of no one listening to me, there is going to be an explosion and the victims' blood will be on your hands!" Joe said loudly as he slammed his hand down on the desk.

The operative leaned forward.

"Listen to me, you shit. Leave now or I will have you arrested under the Terrorism Act. Do yourself a favour, go back to the shit hole you crawled from and keep taking whatever it is you lot take. Don't pester us again!"

Joe was fuming and realised he would need to be more persuasive if he was to be heard.

He left the station before the threat of arrest could be put into action. He left more annoyed with their constant lack of interest, more so than on his previous visit.

Joe found a local phone box and, eventually after calling an enquiry operator, he managed to get through to Steve in the pub.

"Steve. Hi it's Joe."

"Oh my God Joe. It's great to hear from you. How have you been?"

"I'm OK, thanks. I hope you guys have all been OK too? How's Julia?"

"Yeah, we're all fine here, Joe. Nothing ever changes. Julia is OK too and things seemed to have calmed down at home. We all often talk about you, and you know she still misses you?"

"I think there is going to be an attack on the Changing of the Guard in Windsor. I have tried telling the police and they threw me out of the station."

"Surely, the police would know about it already?"

"No, I overheard a conversation by chance, that's how I know about it."

"Are you sure you're OK, Joe?"

"Of course I'm alright. Why is no-one listening to me?"

"Would you like to come and see us? You sound agitated."

"No. I am trying to tell you as your place is right on the route of the daily parade. Tell the police, Steve. Tell them they will have an attack soon."

There was a small pause.

"I know. Don't worry, we'll be OK, Joe, and I will tell Julia you called."

The phone went dead and Joe slammed the receiver down in anger.

He felt so alone in the world with no one to turn to, Only Caelan seemed interested, and even then, only just.

Joe walked slowly back to the cemetery and slipped through the fence. He was sitting on the tomb staring at the wall when Caelan came in and asked Joe if he was OK. He was told of his latest experience with the police.

"Why bother, Joe? I've told you time and time again, they're simply not interested. Let it go, it's probably nothing anyway."

"Fuck this, I need to find out what's going on and tell someone!"

As each day passed, Joe became more agitated until Saturday night finally arrived. He was waiting in the hide when the two planners met.

"So, we're set then?" Mr. F asked.

"Yep, next Saturday."

"And plan B is also in place?"

"Good, just make sure the wind is in the right direction before parking and setting the second ones off."

Joe instantly knew what they were talking about. Initial small incendiary devices followed by a chemical, biological or radiological secondary device. *'God this is going to be big. Seriously big'* Joe thought to himself. He knew that it had the potential to kill people and, if planned with the right logistics in mind, such as location, wind directions and timings, possibly hundreds of thousands of innocent people were going to die.

"Right, no one ever comes here, so leave your car as the secure hide. We can collect it afterwards."

Joe knew he was right. No one had ever come down the small lane as there were no tell-tale signs such as cigarette butts, tissues, needles or condoms as well as grass having taken over the majority of what used to be a small tarmac lane.

The boot of one the cars was opened and various items, which Joe really couldn't identify, started being transferred from one car to the other. Eventually their mobile phones were turned off and thrown in the boot of the car.

The two planners left in Mr. F's car. Joe couldn't believe it. Not only did he now know what was going to happen, but there was potential evidence in the car they had left behind.

He made his way back to wake Caelan with the update.

"What now?" Caelan said, knowing Joe was in a heightened state of excitement.

"You have to seriously listen to me" Joe said loudly as he started to explain everything he had overheard.

"At least we're safe here."

That was not the reaction he was expecting.

"I can't let this go. I need to think about what I can do now."

Joe knew he was on his own to get someone, anyone to listen to him so he called the pub hoping Julia would be working and the one to answer the phone. His luck was in and he heard her sweet voice.

"Hello, the Kings Arms. How may I help you?"

Joe listened to her voice and after what seemed like an eternity, he replied.

"Julia. Hi, it's Joe."

"Oh my God. My sweet baby, how are you?"

"I'm Ok, thanks. I need to tell you something and please, please listen to me."

He told her about the attack, asked her to call the police and not to come into work the following Saturday.

"My God! Steve told me that you called the other day and that you sounded odd. Are you sure you're OK?"

"I swear on my love for you, what I am telling you is the truth. Please believe me."

"I do, Joe. I am just a bit worried about you, that's all."

Joe could sense Steve had corrupted her mind as if to think he was now mentally unstable and had lost the plot.

"Julia, my love, please believe what I have said, keep safe and do not love me any less for what I may have to do."

"Joe..." was the last thing he heard her say as he placed the handset down.

Hearing the voice of the woman he loved again, that alone-in-the-world feeling came over him. A tear ran down his face as he walked away from the phone box.

Joe headed back to the cemetery and noticed the car was still parked as it was left. He broke a piece of old railing from one of the graves and went to the rear of the car, where he managed to prize open the boot.

The car alarm was either not set, or it didn't have one as he stood there for a few seconds expecting it to go off. He found an assortment of clothes and old phones along with two small overnight bags.

He rifled through everything but the only significant items appeared to be the two mobile phones. He took them and slammed down the slightly damaged boot and returned to the safety of the tomb.

"What you up to?" he was asked as he entered.

"I broke into the boot of the car and found these phones."

"Are you fucking nuts?"

"Listen, no one is willing to listen to me, so I will have to make them listen. I need to try to stop the attacks, Caelan."

"Joe. You need to really think about this. You could end up in a whole pile of crap. Not only are you going around scaring people, but now breaking into people's cars!"

"I know what I am doing" Joe said as he started to try to turn on the phones.

The phones were numerically password protected, but he was sure that the information would still be contained on the SIM card memory for the proper authorities to check.

The next morning, with only a few days left to the attack, Joe seemed in a different world. He was just staring at the wall of the tomb contemplating his next move and, after some time, came around but then realised Caelan wasn't there.

He must be on one of his scavenging patrols he thought to himself as he calmly made a small fire and brewed a tea. It wasn't until he went back into the tomb to get out of the small rain shower that he noticed Caelan's stuff was missing.

He searched the tomb and their store areas and established that he had done a bunk. Eventually he found a small note saying. *Joe. Mate, please forgive me for leaving but I am worried about you and what you could be getting into. If you need me, you know where to find me. Take care, mate and be safe.'* Joe felt even more alone than before. He had nothing now, only the information he had in his head and that which was hopefully stored on the two phones he now had in his possession.

He packed his stuff in a plastic bag along with his wallet and key to Gaby's house, and hid it in his own safe location, under the slab of his daily visited VC holder's grave. After all, if he couldn't trust him with it, who could he trust?

He started walking back into the centre of London. He knew what he had to do now.

He took his time, passing by the same landmarks he and Caelan had passed on their new adventure some months previous. *'How life can change in such a short space of time'* he thought to himself.

He slept in the same spot in Regents Park under a large, thick bush, and although it was as safe as anywhere he could find in the open, it was a restless night knowing he had to do something to get people to listen.

Time was running out and he needed to seriously think of his next move. He didn't know what he was going to do, but he knew that he had to do something, but whatever he did, he needed to make people listen.

He quickly washed in the lake and started to walk past Broadcasting House, Piccadilly Circus and Trafalgar Square. He took in all the sites he remembered when his life seemed complete and he enjoyed the social scenes of London from Chelsea to the West End.

He watched ordinary people in love. People with children and tourists excited to be in the capital of the great nation he was once so proud to defend. All the people around him seemed content; they were happy, and appeared to have nothing to worry about. If only they knew of the future catastrophe about to ruin their existence, to ruin everyone's lives across the country. It played on Joe's mind like never before and he felt sad. With a heavy heart, he made his way along Whitehall and stopped at the gates of Downing Street, where he managed to make his way easily through the small tourist crowds surrounding the gate.

He looked through the black railings to see an armed Police Officer patrolling from right to left just a few feet away. He knew they were better trained and more intelligent than the average plod in the station or on the streets and, if anyone was going to listen to him, it was someone from the armed Diplomatic Protection Division of the Metropolitan Police. He had worked with them in the past when taking part in various military processions through the Capital.

He knew this was the right thing to do, and didn't hesitate. "Hey, pal!"

The Armed Officer turned and faced him slightly raising his German Heckler and Koch MP5 semi-automatic machinegun.

"Listen, I have these phones I need to you take and show the Counter Terrorist Unit" Joe shouted as he raised both phones in one hand.

The weapon was now raised to chest height as the Officer moved back two paces and radioed for assistance. When as another two armed officers ran forward with rifles at the aim, the crowd at the gates ran for safety and, only Joe was left standing there.

"Sir, move away from the gate."

"I can't. I need you to listen to me, please. I am aware of an attack that is going to happen this Saturday."

"Sir, listen to me, we are armed and will use force if necessary. Place the phones on the floor and take a step backwards."

Joe could now hear sirens in the background. He knew he needed to make not just the police, but the higher authorities listen about the potential threat, no matter what it took. His life didn't matter anymore. "I am going to throw the phones towards you. Please look at them.

They have all the evidence you need to stop it."

"Sir, don't throw the phones. Place them on the floor and step back or we will open fire. I repeat, place the phones on the floor or we will have no option but to open fire."

Joe reached into his pocket with his free hand, felt for the old penny he had been given by Julia, held it tight, then closed his eyes. He saw the love of his life's face and whispered a last farewell.

"I love you. Please be safe."

He threw the phones towards the officers who had their weapons trained on him.

He heard the shot and felt himself being knocked off of his feet. Joe's body hit the floor and he lay there feeling the warm loss of blood flowing from his body and slowly losing consciousness.

He saw an outline of a person kneeling in front of him, and only managed to say Julia's name again before he felt nothing else and faded away.

REALITY COMES AT A COST

J oe started to come around and found himself surrounded by what appeared to be medical and police personnel through his blurred vision.

Some of their words eventually started to make sense.

"Can you hear me Joe?" the nearest white-coated, male with round spectacles said.

Joe tried to get his words out, but seemed to mumble rather than talk as his mouth seemed incapable of moving.

"OK lay there and try to get some rest. We'll be back later."

The group seemed to disperse, and Joe could only make out two people, one a shadow in the corner of the room but he recognised the chequered blocks of a police band. The other shadow moved slowly towards him.

"Joe, it's me. Are you OK?"

He didn't immediately recognise the voice.

"Do you know where you are?" the female voice asked.

Still unable to talk, he tried to shake his head, but couldn't move, and felt excruciating pain run through his body. Everything went black again as he lost consciousness.

Joe woke some days later. His vision eventually coming back, and he could see an armed Police Officer standing at the back of the room.

He slowly took his surroundings in and eventually realised that he was in a secure room in some sort of medical facility.

The Police Officer, realising he was conscious, went to the door and opened it slightly. He spoke to an unknown person on the other side that Joe couldn't see. He closed the door and without saying anything, took the same stance in the room he had when Joe had first woken.

The room quickly filled with people, from doctors, nurses and two suited males whom Joe presumed to be the police. A male in a white coat leaned forward.

"Joe. You are in St Michaels Hospital. Can you hear me OK?"

Joe managed to nod, but his throat was sore and it hurt to try. "Good. My name is Doctor Simon Davitt. You have been shot and have been in and out of consciousness for the last two weeks. You are OK but you needed a couple of operations as the bullet entered your upper left chest area."

The doctor went on to explain in medical terms what he had been through and what was needed for his rehabilitation. Joe took some, but not all, of the information in. The doctor moved to one side and one of the suited men walked forward.

"I am Chief Inspector Ryan from the Counter Terrorist Unit of the Metropolitan Police. Your actions, although they were extreme, helped save many lives. Unfortunately, not all of the devices were found in time, and we did suffer some fatal casualties. We will need your help in identifying those responsible for the planning and executing the attack."

Joe felt relieved that eventually someone had listened to him, and his mind wandered whilst he was listening to the voice that was saying something but nothing.

"I think we should leave him to rest now" the doctor said.

They left the room as quickly as they had entered apart from one nurse.

"Relax and try to rest now. We will be back later, but sleep if you can."

Joe looked at her and all he could do was to nod.

She was a nice-looking woman with bobbed, blond hair and had a soft, warming voice. He lay there and wondered how Julia was and how she would now look at him not only for being homeless, but being shot by the police. He had no chance with her, if he ever had one. He soon fell asleep to let his body recover.

He felt someone slightly shaking his arm and could hear the familiar, soft voice again.

"Joe. We need to take the tube out of your mouth and make you more comfortable."

Joe nodded as he became more aware of the same nurse leaning over him with another colleague. They removed the feeding tube, and he spluttered as they withdrew the long see-through, thin pipeline and raised the supporting back part of the bed in order to help him sit slightly up.

He could now see clearly and the Police Officer in the room wasn't looking at him at all, only at the door and occasionally at the window which, although the light was shining through, had its blinds closed.

Joe tried to talk, but felt as though he had eaten half of the Sahara Desert.

"How long have I been in here?"

"Just over two weeks." the nurse said as Joe made the name on the badge she wore as Sarah.

"Can I have some water please?"

Sarah helped him sip the water and he felt her close to his side. He missed being near someone, the warmth of a touch, and the soft feel of a hand; he missed Julia.

"Can I use a phone?"

The nurse looked at the Officer who looked at her, and shook his head.

"I'm sorry, Joe. We can't let you just yet" she replied as she continued about her duties.

Joe was feeling much more responsive and alert, despite a slight tightening in the chest. He asked the nurse to show him his injuries and she helped him move his gown to one side.

He could see very little as he looked down, but he could see the line where the stitches used to be, and a small patch of deformed skin, presumably where the entry point of the bullet had been.

"See, it's not too bad" Sarah went on to confirm.

He knew he was lucky to be alive and, in one way, he was grateful but in another, he wished he had joined his three friends for the guilt he carried around every day.

The following week saw him become physically and mentally stronger. Apart from the medical staff that visited him regularly, he did not speak to anyone else. Not even the officers in the room, who changed over regularly, spoke to him. He thought this was odd but, after all, they were the police and he remembered how they had treated him in the past, not to mention them shooting him.

"You have a visitor" Sarah said on one of the daily checks she performed. Joe was sitting on the side of the bed and smiling to himself, as he waited for Julia to come through the door, but it was Gaby that walked in and his smile slipped away from his face.

"Joe. Thank God you're OK" she said as she went to hug him.

He tried to stop her as he pointed to his chest, which didn't make any difference as she embraced him and he moved slightly in pain.

"We were so worried about you."

She explained she had been working and had been told by her manager, whom he had met, that he had been shot in Downing Street by the police as a suspected terrorist. She couldn't believe it and wondered where he had been over the last few months.

The report on the television had been that an unknown male had tried to blow up the Prime Minister, and she couldn't believe it when his name was mentioned as the suspect.

She sat with Joe for over an hour chatting about what she had been up to since he left. She explained that she had been told by the police not to discuss the details with him about the attacks. Despite this information, he still kept asking and glancing over at the officer.

"If I go against what they have asked, I could be arrested."

"What! That's mad."

"Hey, Officer, why is no one telling me anything?" but in their usual fashion, the Officer headed to the door and left the room for a split second before returning to his position without saying anything.

A few minutes later, a familiar-looking male entered the room. "I am not sure if you remember me?"

"I am Chief Inspector Ryan. I believe you have been asking questions relating to the attacks."

"I have to be honest with you, Joe, we do not know what your involvement in all of this has been."

"What the fuck are you saying?" Joe said in disbelief.

"We are still gathering the facts, and we need to be sure what part you played in this, if at all. At this time, we are waiting to formally interview you."

"You are kidding me right?"

"Well you did mention terrorist attack and threw two objects at an armed police officer."

"Anyway, there will be plenty of time for this later. Get some rest." He left Joe laying there with Gaby holding his hand.

Joe was stunned with what he had just heard, and he didn't know whether to get up and chase after him or do a runner from the hospital.

Joe was eventually calmed down by his sister, but remained frustrated that he was not allowed to know anything about the attacks that he had tried to save, as well as now being accused of being one of the spineless terrorists that had attacked the UK. The same country he had put his life on the line for, time after time.

As time passed, his wounds healed and he was eventually told by the doctor that he would be released into police custody within the next forty-eight hours.

"What do you mean custody?"

"The police want to talk to you regarding the incident that led to your shooting" the doctor replied.

Eventually, Chief Inspector Ryan made a re-appearance and pulled up a chair and ordered the armed officer to leave the room.

"OK, Joe. I want you to listen very carefully to me. We now know that you had nothing to do with the attacks and that you had previously tried making the authorities aware of the information you had gathered. We are dealing with those people as I talk."

Joe sat listening.

"We need your help, Joe. It's as simple as that. We need to find those who planned this as fast as we can before they get another opportunity to strike again."

"Why should I help you now?"

"I didn't want to tell you, but your sister helped us confirm that you know some of those killed in the blast in Windsor."

"I believe you know the landlord, his wife and the bar staff at the Kings Arms?" he asked.

Joe nodded as he lowered his head knowing what was to come.

The pub had taken the side blast of the explosion and killed Steve and Maureen outright. Some of those injured were bar staff, luckily near the back of the bar area."

"Please tell me Julia wasn't killed?"

"Julia Nightingale was one of those injured but she only suffered minor injuries."

Joe felt a tear trickle down his face and a deep, heavy pain in his heart. It was his fault. He had tried to stop it but no one had listened.

Maybe he should have done something else, something more to convince them. *'This is Afghanistan all over again'* he thought to himself.

"We would first of all like you to work with us to try to identify those responsible. Once we know who they are and have them in custody, we would like to place you into the newly formed Witness Protection Service."

"What does that mean?"

Ryan went through the details which initially involved working with him and his team. Once they had identified and arrested the planners, Joe would go into hiding within the protection service where he would be re-housed, set up with a job, given £80 per week and given a new identity.

"This is something out of a spy novel!"

"We take this seriously Joe, but there is another condition. You can't see, or communicate, with anyone you know. Anyone!"

"Can I take someone with me?"

"Yes. We allow dependents and spouses."

"What if I wanted to take someone else?"

"Who are you thinking of?"

"Julia" he confirmed as Ryan looked blank for a short time.

"But she's married."

"I know, but what if she agreed, could I be allowed?"

"That's not allowed, Joe."

"OK if you don't even ask her, or let me, then the deal is off and you can find the planners on your own."

Joe went on, for the first time in his life, to tell a complete stranger how much Julia meant to him, and how they had built upon on their relationship over a short period of time. Ryan understood as he had been married to his wife for 23 years and he loved her desperately. Joe felt relieved being able to openly talk about her and his feelings.

FORGET THE PAST

The knock on the door startled Julia as she lay on the sofa, watching trash TV as she had done since being released from hospital. After unlocking and opening the door, she stood looking blankly as this unknown, smartly-dressed male who came forward to greet her.

"Julia Nightingale? My name is Chief Inspector Ryan" he confirmed by producing his black, leather-covered warrant card.

"May I come in please?"

Julia sat back on the sofa and turned off the TV as Ryan quickly looked around the very clean and orderly room and sat on the chair to her side.

"Julia, you don't mind if I call you Julia do you?"

"No, that's fine."

"I am here to discuss something with you which you must never repeat to anyone. Do you understand?"

"Err... I think so."

"You know Joe Forrester, is that correct?"

After receiving a nod of acceptance to the question, he went on to ask more probing questions about how well she knew him and her thoughts about their relationship. Further questions regarding what she thought of him now, and when the last time she had seen him were asked to confirm what Joe had already told him.

Ryan was satisfied with what he had heard and it was obvious she loved Joe.

"OK. Here's the reason for me coming. Joe may be going into a witness protection programme with our help."

Ryan went on to explain what it meant for Joe, how Joe felt about Julia, and spending the rest of his life with her under new identities.

"He would like you to go with him. We are aware that you are married and, of course, the choice is yours. I realise that you may need time to think about it so here's my card. Call me soon, please."

"My husband won't let me go."

"He doesn't need to know. We can arrange various scenarios for you to ensure he will never be able to see or trace you again. You will be entirely safe."

"Can you guarantee that?"

"Yes, I can. It is foolproof and very few people within the police will know who you both are, where you have moved to and your new names." Julia cried as she thought of everything that had happened since they had last seen each other. She still loved him with every breath, and her situation at home had not changed with the occasional mental and physical pain her husband inflicted upon her, and she knew Joe would never harm her.

"OK, I'll do it."

"Oh. OK" Ryan said in surprise, as he had not expected her to respond so quickly and positively.

He explained what she needed to do in preparation for her departure on a date to be agreed. Ryan left as quickly as he had arrived, and Julia was left with a light at the end of her very dark, gloomy domestic, loveless tunnel.

Joe was sitting dressed and waiting for Ryan to re-appear as the expected knock on the door happened.

The armed officer opened the door only to be met with the end of a double barreled shotgun shoved in his face. The weapon exploded causing the officers face to implode as he was hurled back across the room.

Joe instinctively jumped up and grabbed the end of the barrel trying to fight off the attacker who was of equal size. Joe dropped his assailant using his unarmed fighting skills to inflict a deadly blow to his windpipe.

The attacker went down with a thud as Joe kept hold of the barrel end of the weapon. He quickly turned it, and aimed the remaining loaded barrel at the second masked gunman standing in shock in the corridor at the sight of his partner in crime being killed.

Joe's eyes quickly glanced at the dead officer in the chair outside of the door and, without hesitation, released the remaining cartridge at the groin of the second attacker. He hit the back wall and fell to the floor, but not before his blood splattered across the walls. As he lay there, his life poured away from his still body. The attackers were no more.

Joe shouted to the nurse at the station at the end of the corridor. "Call the police immediately and get some medics here now!"

Joe opened and unclipped the dead officer's issued Glock pistol, removed the spare and full magazines from the pouches on his belt, and repeated the process to the faceless officer in the room before heading towards the staircase as his flight survival instinct kicked in.

He needed to escape any further potential attacks which may have been planned.

Joe concealed the pistols in his jacket and headed towards the ambulance bay. He found a small room that had been left unlocked and entered. He stood behind the closed door taking in what had just happened. He needed to get away, and fast, in case there were any more of them. He slid out of the loading bay and made his way through the mall roads that led away from the main entrance and headed towards the nearest tube station.

He had never leapt over the barriers before, but he had no cash and therefore no choice. He made his way towards Archway watching every person, their movements, and all of the time he had a hand on one of the concealed pistols. He couldn't trust anyone any longer.

He was again on his own relying on his survival instincts and training.

Sneaking away from the station, he made his way to the concealed entrance to the cemetery that he had so often used to ensure he was not seen entering or leaving. The items he had stored under the grave were still there. Now he had money and weapons, and he began to feel more comfortable that he could defend himself.

He entered the tomb and immediately pulled the pistol to the firing position as he noticed a lone figure in the corner.

"What the fuck!" was Caelan's response to having a pistol aimed at him.

"God, it's you. What are you doing back here scaring the crap out of me?"

"Oddly enough, I noticed you were otherwise engaged under her Majesty's protection so, I came back here. It's still the best homeless house I've ever had" he said with humour in his voice, until Joe explained what had recently occurred.

"Shit, Joe. I'm really sorry for not believing you in the first place, mate. What can I do to help? You name it" he stated.

Joe had already had the basics of a plan.

"I need to get to Julia and bring her back here. She is not safe now, especially as we have been compromised. This is the only safe place I know and where I can protect her."

"They know your face, Joe. Why not stay here and I'll go get her?" Caelan suggested.

Joe thought about it for a few minutes then reluctantly agreed and gave him the money contained in his wallet, her address, the second pistol and spare magazines just in case. After all he was going to protect Julia until they were back in the safety of the tomb, and he needed to know that he had everything necessary to bring her back to him.

"Remember how to use one of these?"

"Dick!" was the only response he got before Caelan left.

Joe soon got to work setting traps. If anyone crossed the fishing wire, it would automatically knock over a pile of tin cans alarming Joe to someone's presence. Simple, but effective, and at least he could be ready to kill his attackers if he needed to.

He sat and waited above the tombs in a prone position, out of the view of any potential intruders and, although it was cold, the adrenalin was still rushing around his body.

Caelan waited across the street for some time before deciding to go and knock on the door.

As he started walking towards the house, he noticed a couple leaving and realised it must be Julia and her husband.

"Bollocks" he said out loudly.

This was not part of his plan, and he had to think fast.

He ran across the road towards them as they were getting into their car.

"Julia?" he asked as he stood next to her.

"Who the fuck are you?" her husband said with anger in his voice as he started to make his way around to the passenger side of the vehicle. Caelan had taken them by surprise and ignored him.

"You have to come with me now, Julia."

"Hey, shit head. Get out of here before I..." he was stopped dead in his tracks as the Glock was aimed at his face.

"Do yourself a favour, pal, and fuck off right now" Caelan ordered and, without hesitation, Mike ran towards the front door.

"Joe sent me and you have to come now. You and Joe are in real danger. He said you would know he sent me as he told me to tell you that you have his rock climber and he has your old penny, whatever that means?"

She stood frozen for a few seconds, and the shock that had taken over her body would stay for a long time to come, but Caelan shook her arm gently.

"Come on, we have to go right now."

She nodded and they swiftly walked away down the dimly lit suburban street.

Rather than heading directly for the railway station, they caught a street cab to the next station along the line. That way if her husband had called the police, they would be waiting at the local station for them.

They sat at the far end of the platform waiting for the next train. The train seemed to take forever and Julia remained silent for the majority of the time.

"Is Joe alright?"

"Oh, he's a fighter that one. He's OK. You'll be with him soon enough."

The train arrived and Caelan hesitated as he held onto Julia's arm, pulling her back before heading to the carriage making sure they were not followed.

The train journey was spent with silence and suspicion before they eventually pulled into Waterloo.

The constant flow of passengers allowed them to mingle with the crowd and leave through one of the small archways leading past the Eurostar entrance.

Turning down small, pedestrian tunnels that spread under the roads above, they came out on the other side of the main road passing by the station and its bottle-neck main approaches, and the hundreds of commuters going about their business unaware of their presence. They hailed another cab.

Caelan asked the driver to stop about half a mile from the cemetery and departed from the vehicle in a residential street.

"We have to walk from here."

They stopped opposite their own entrance to see if anyone was watching or nearby, and, once he was happy that it was clear, they entered the cemetery. Caelan went down on one knee tugging at Julia to do the same.

"Right, you have to be mega quiet in here. No one knows we're here and Joe will be waiting for us, but we need to be quiet and quick. OK?" Julia nodded and they got to their feet and moved towards the circle.

He stopped slightly before the entrance to the circle and gave their coded noise. He then entered slowly and noticed the fish wire stretched across the path. As he stepped over it, he turned to Julia and indicated for her to do the same.

Joe spotted them from his hidden location and immediately looked further past them in all directions to see if they had been followed, but there were no signs of unwanted intruders.

He climbed down from the roof of the tomb and waited outside their hide-out. He saw Julia and ran towards her as she did him. They embraced tightly as if they should never have been apart. Joe held her arms and looked at her in the eyes.

"My sweet, beautiful woman, I have missed you so, so much." She was crying and Joe could also feel himself welling up.

They entered the tomb as Caelan stayed outside waiting to ensure they were alone. Joe explained everything that had happened in sequence, from his sister, being beaten up, becoming homeless to the death of the police officers. Julia was trembling with fear.

"Are we really in danger, Joe?"

"Yes, but I swear, I will protect you, don't worry, we'll be OK." He assured her as he embraced her again as Caelan entered.

"OK. So what's the plan now that we have alienated the remainder of the population, fought off Bin-shit head and his pals and got two policemen killed?" he asked as though he had been by Joe's side throughout.

Caelan had always had an odd sense of humour and it was certainly needed now.

"I need to contact Ryan and get some assurances from him as to our safety as we can't stay here too long. I need to try to call him. Have you still got some money left?"

"Yeah, thirty quid."

"OK, head to the local supermarket and buy a pay-as-you-go phone. Top it up and get back here sharpish. We need to start making plans ASAP, oh, and Caelan, thank you, pal."

He gave Joe a slight grin indicating *'I'm right here with you, all the way'* as he left the area once again.

Both of them had gone straight back into military mode and knowing each-others movements and plans helped them achieve their goals in half the time.

Julia had handed over Ryan's business card she had been carrying around with her since he had visited.

When Caelan returned, the tomb was empty. He placed the charged-up phone behind the raised tomb and stepped outside. He felt the cold steel of the pistol against the side of his head.

"Sorry" Joe said as he lowered the gun.

"It's getting a bit of a habit now" Caelan joked as they re-entered the tomb.

"How did you manage to charge it?"

"Err... it's called a 24 hour café in the supermarket and, funny enough, they appear to have plug sockets, and real electricity too."

"Sorry. Good thinking Batman."

"So what's the next step?"

Julia was curled up on the tomb and Joe placed his jacket over her. "Baby, we'll just be outside, I promise you, I am going nowhere without you. Sleep well, my love" he said as they went outside.

"OK. Joking aside, what the fuck are we going to do now?"

"I need to chat to Ryan and take things from there."

He tried the phone and it kept ringing.

He checked the number again on the card to that on the phone and tried it again. The same constant ringing was becoming annoying.

On the third attempt, the phone was picked up. "Hello" the person answering said.

Joe didn't recognise the voice.

"Hello. Who am I speaking to please?"

"This is Ryan. How may I help you?"

Joe was suspicious, it didn't sound like him.

"I need to ask you something first. What's the woman's name if the male is called Joe?"

"Joe, is that you? Where are you? Let me come and get you" he said in a flustered voice.

"The name of the woman first!"

There was a slight hesitation in the unknown voice. "Of course. It's Helen."

Joe cancelled the call immediately.

"That wasn't Ryan who answered his mobile."

Joe thought for a few minutes wondering who else he could trust. "Gaby, it's me, I need to meet you. Don't say anything, but look for the last place Karl Marx visited dead or alive and I'll be there, tomorrow at 11am. Don't tell anyone and come alone. I will find you."

He cancelled the call.

Joe knew she would turn up, that she would have to join the tourist group and then sneak off, but then he began to wonder if she knew what he meant. She wasn't stupid and surely she could figure it out, he just hoped she hadn't been drinking, and that she could hear the urgency in his voice.

Julia slept well considering her trauma over the last few hours. Caelan, who could sleep on a washing line, slept heavily, but Joe on the other hand couldn't sleep and kept guard all night above the tomb, never once taking his hand off of the Glock.

Sunrise was extraordinarily beautiful and, although there was a slight chill and frost in the air, Joe appreciated the beauty of each day, especially at the moment not knowing if it was going to be his last, but more importantly now that Julia was with him.

He wondered how long they would sleep for and although he wanted to wake them, he knew they would need as much rest as they could get.

Caelan was the first to wake and exit the tomb.

"Morning, you" Joe said as he leaned over the side of the tomb to tap him on the head.

"For fuck's sake Joe, stop bloody trying to give me a heart attack."

"Sorry. Just couldn't sleep."

"I think Julia needs to have some food inside of her, and as your ugly mug is probably in all the papers at the moment, I don't mind going as I'm starving too" Caelan said.

It was agreed between them that he would head to the nearest fast food place that would be open to grab some food. Neither of them knew what the day had in store, but they knew they would need all the energy they could get.

THE CALL

fter eating what can only be described as junk food breakfast, all three sat around the inside of the tomb. Julia had never looked so lovely to Joe, but she was paranoid about how she looked and the state of her hair.

"Trust me, baby, we'll get this sorted today. I need to leave you with Caelan for a while later but, trust me, it's something I need to do for us all."

"You promised me you wouldn't leave me again, Joe."

"I'm not leaving you. I will be right here, well nearby in the cemetery."

"Err... Hello. I am here you know!"

Caelan started waving his hands around as if he was waving to an imaginary friend.

Joe was already in hiding when the tour started.

"Here on the right, we find Karl Heinrich Marx's grave. As one can see, it is an imposing monument for a truly inspiring Prussian Philosopher, renowned for his founding of Marxism which fought for workers' equality" said the elderly, registered blue-badge tour guide.

Joe could see, from his position between the trees and heavy foliage behind the grave, Gaby's figure. He watched as they all took turns in having their photos taken in front of the monument pointing to the famous words inscribed '**Workers of all lands unite**.'

The tour eventually moved away and Gaby quickly manoeuvered herself behind the large monument, hiding from the remainder of the group as they meandered along the small pathway.

She stayed there for what seemed like an eternity, but it was only long enough for Joe to ensure she wasn't being watched or followed. Joe moved towards her, his hand again on the Glock. He stood with his back to the rear of the monument as Gaby was on the side.

"Gaby, don't look around or hesitate but follow me" he said as they both disappeared into the foliage.

"God, Joe, I heard what happened, what is going on?"

"I'm not sure, but I need you to do something for me. I know we have had our differences and for those I am sorry. I need to try to contact a Chief Inspector Ryan from the Counter Terrorist Unit of the Met."

"What can I do if you already know him?"

"I think his phone may be compromised, but can you try to covertly track him down for me through your contacts with the council?"

"Joe, I'm not sure I can."

"If you don't we're all dead. He is the only one that can help us and the only person that seems to want to help us, but I'm not sure if he has been removed, if you know what I mean?"

Joe asked Gaby that if she managed to contact him to arrange a meet locally, and he went on to describe him, just in case another person arrived instead.

"OK, Joe. I'll do it but I'm bloody nervous."

"Welcome to my world, Sis, but call me on the number I phoned you on earlier after you find out what you can. Be careful, Gaby, and please don't tell anyone, including Ryan, where we met or that we think someone is onto us. This is serious shit Sis, and I really can't do this without you."

They quickly hugged and she left as swiftly as she had arrived to catch up with the rest of the group.

Joe waited for a short time before heading back to the circle and, as he did so, he was trying to rack his brains as what their next move would be if Ryan wasn't around. George was the only other person in an official capacity he could trust, but he knew he would only contact him if he really had to. He decided to wait for Gaby's call.

The remainder of the day was spent discussing the situation and their potential options.

"Why can't we just go to the police station?" Julia asked.

"We can't. Been there, done that one I am afraid."

She knew the options were limited and felt nervous. A tear rolled down her face. Caelan nodded to Joe to look at her and as he did he put his arm around her.

"Come on, baby. It will all be OK once we chat to Ryan. We'll soon all be sitting in a bar laughing about this, you watch."

Joe, for the first time, had to lie to her.

Julia placed her head on his chest and fell asleep.

The day seemed to drag by and Joe was becoming impatient as he waited for the call. Yet again, he was the only one awake. He couldn't sleep and reflected on the two armed officers that had lost their lives protecting him. It felt weird as he was used to, having to fight in operational zones, not on the streets of London.

They had two pistols and spare magazines but, against the attackers who were armed with more powerful weapons, they stood little chance unless they used their tactical advantage to get through this, at least both he and Caelan had similar skills and operational experience.

"What do you want to do, Joe?"

"I don't know, but the more isolated the location the better to give us time."

"I was thinking of grabbing a car and some cash and heading away sharpish."

"What's this place then if not remote?" Caelan asked with surprise.

Joe explained their only option, if Gaby or Ryan had been compromised, was to get as far away as possible from the cemetery as it would only be a matter of time before they figured out the mobile number and tracked its location.

"We need to think fast and be ready to leave at a moment's notice. Right, I'll get the cash and car, you stay here and look after Julia, if you're OK with that?"

Joe got the nod again from his comrade in arms confirming the plan.

Joe left as it became dark and headed towards the town. He knew he would have to think on his feet as he walked.

He called Gaby again. A male voice answered the phone and it took Joe by surprise

"Where's Gaby?"

"She is right here with us and if you want to see her alive again, you will come here within the next hour."

"Who the fuck are you and what do you want?"

"We can discuss that when you get here."

Joe knew he couldn't risk going there under any circumstances. "Why not come and meet me instead?"

"Listen you. I'm not messing around here, get your arse over here within the hour. Oh, and to prove we're serious, let me give you a taste of what will happen if you don't."

Joe heard the thud of a silenced pistol and Gaby's screams echoed down the line. The phone went dead.

The small caliber round had entered Gaby's hand as it was being held against the table, shattering and splintering the bones from her wrist to the base of her fingers as it tore through the muscles, ligaments and veins and blood started to flow on the table. The scream was from the base of her stomach as she felt the burning pain spreading up her arm. She could feel herself crying as the assailant thumped her so hard in the abdomen, she fell to the floor unconscious.

Joe was taken aback. He had now got his sister injured if not killed. He felt even more guilt and now didn't know what to do. He had promised Julia he would look after her, and now his sister was in serious trouble too, he could only think of one thing to do and dialed 141 followed by 999.

"There are armed intruders who have just shot someone."

He knew that call would spark off an armed response unit notification, and he gave the address and cut the call short. There was nothing else he could do to try to help Gaby. He had to clear his head and get them away from London right now.

Standing in front of the cash machine, he knew that once he made a withdrawal the authorities would know exactly where he was, that was of course, if it was in fact them after them! He took out the maximum amount available for the day and headed towards the small row of shops.

He stood in the doorway for some time watching the cash machine from a distance. He knew he needed a vehicle, but if he hijacked one, it would be reported immediately. He had to take one that gave them a time advantage and the ones parked around the shops were not an option. After a short while he headed to a quiet residential street.

He stopped on the corner to tear off a small length of branch from a tree which lined the street. It was only about three feet long but should be good enough for what he needed. As he walked he removed all the foliage from the branch, so all he had was a stick with a small Y fork at the top. As he continued to walk along the street, he looked for a car big enough for all three of them and powerful enough to get away at speed if needed.

Towards the centre of the road, he noticed one of the street lights was out and a dark four-wheel drive vehicle parked in one of the sloping driveways. The house, a 70's style, porch-fronted building had no internal lights on, which hopefully indicated the residents were either out or had gone to bed. Joe moved towards the front door and quietly lifted the letterbox. His intuition paid off.

The car keys were hanging on a small hook opposite the door with various other bunches of keys. Joe slowly slid the branch through and aimed the fork end towards the keys he wanted. It took him a couple of tries but eventually he had hooked the keys and pulled them slowly towards the letterbox. Having them, he sat crouched by the side of the porch and pressed the unlock button the on the remote control.

He waited to see if anyone had been alerted to his actions of unlocking the car, and when he was satisfied, he slid in the driver's seat, placed the keys in the ignition without turning over the engine and released the handbrake. The car moved forward under its own weight off the driveway and, when it was some feet away from the house, Joe started the engine and slowly drove away towards the cemetery.

He stopped a couple of streets away and checked the drawers and doors for anything he may need. A SatNav, a handheld torch and a UK atlas were the only useful things apart from a bag of humbug mints. He took the atlas and the small torch, locked the vehicle and entered the cemetery in the usual fashion.

Joe met Caelan outside the tomb and he told him of his actions. They sat in the tomb flicking through the atlas to decide where they needed to go, but within the timescale of the vehicle being reported as stolen.

"OK, we've got eight hours max I rekon before they will know it's been taken."

"Judging that we travel at an average of 50 miles an hour that should give us a 400 mile lead" Caelan said.

They judged on the map of the UK that North would be easier, and eventually after a few minutes Joe pointed to a small village he knew well in Nottinghamshire.

"I know this village and it's right in the sticks with shit-loads of good hiding places, plus I know some people there we can trust."

"That's that then."

Joe woke Julia who looked shattered. At least she could sleep in the car and, although he was tired, he knew he had to stay awake to get them away from London fast.

The Motorway was as it usually was at night. Light of traffic, apart from the never-ending articulated lorries, transporting goods across the network of roads to reach their destinations before the shops opened in the morning to service the nation. He knew he had to stop at one of the services to fill the car and grab some coffee to keep him awake.

The service station was still open, and whilst Joe filled the car with Julia asleep on the back seat, Caelan headed into the main shopping area. When he eventually came back to the car Joe could see some larger items tucked under his arms.

"You'll never guess what they had in there?"

He had picked up some folding chairs and a couple of tents they had on special offer.

"That's excellent mate, we may need them."

He went back to get the coffee and some food for the remainder of the journey, during which Julia would remain asleep.

Turning off at the junction Joe was happy to see the back of the motorway. He headed past the power station he knew well to take the turning towards Barton in Fabis. The small, single track road wound around until he saw the familiar looking farm. He pulled in to the main yard and drove through the hanger which housed the large industrial machinery used on the farm.

He parked in the far corner, well hidden from view of any passing early morning workers. His travel companions were still asleep and Joe, feeling more comfortable now they were outside of London, joined them in getting some well-earned rest.

The knock on the window startled them all, and as Joe went for the pistol he immediately recognised one of Simon's sons, Will, and he slid the pistol back under his seat.

"Hey Joe, didn't know you were coming up."

"Hi, Will, just thought I'd surprise you all and I brought some friends with me."

"Mum and Dad are up, want some tea?" he offered on their behalf.

The house hadn't changed over the years and stood alone from the main farm area overlooking the valley below.

It had been built on the site of an old monastery, and Simon had often told stories of the original secret passageways still being used today leading to and from the monastery, originally for the monks to evade capture and impending death at the hands of Henry VIII; usually in a drunken stupor.

He would offer to show Joe, and those being entertained, the last surviving tunnels which he had attempted to restore over the years. Of course they were never seen, despite people, including Joe, looking for them when Simon fell asleep in his usual, casual chair after numerous bottles of beer. He became renowned for such tall, historical 'white lies' and became his own 'keeper' of the tunnels, and even George, his old friend, who had been there many times with him pretended to know the entrances just to keep Simon going.

After opening the front door, which always remained unlocked and greeting them both, it felt good seeing some friendly faces at last, as they all sat around the kitchen table.

It had been a long time since Joe had been there, and he recalled George coming with him on the last visit. They had always had a great time, and they had all exchanged phone numbers as George offered them the use of his holiday home in Turkey, but it never came to pass due to the work on the farm being ever-consuming.

Simon, Jane, Will and their other son, Sam, were good honest hard-working people who all worked on the farm or the adjoining farm shop. Joe had known them for a number of years since asking them initially for their help on a task in the local area, and he had instantly liked them and had always trusted them.

Seeing them reminded him of why he liked them. It was as if he had seen them the week before rather than the actual time that had passed, and they greeted him as such.

No questions were asked and no information was offered until the boys went to work. Jane was opening the shop later in the morning and asked to speak with Joe alone.

"Joe, I know what happened. It's been all over the press. Are you OK?"

"Jane, we're in serious trouble. I think someone is out to kill us, that's obvious from the hospital, and now not only has the one copper we trusted gone missing, but they have my sister Gaby. I am seriously running out of options and didn't know where else to go."

He didn't need reminding, he already knew, but she went on to comfort him that they would not be telling anyone of their visit, and they could stay there as long as needed. Joe also knew the boys had a variety of shotguns should they need them. He felt at ease for a short time. Joe returned to the kitchen and it was good seeing Julia looking a bit more like herself.

"Come on you. Let's get you sorted, the boys can wait" Jane said as she took Julia upstairs as Joe and Caelan sat there looking at each other. "I can't believe the last few days, but at least I have Julia and you with me" Joe said as Caelan smiled.

"It's nice to be trusted again, Joe, and I'm with you all the way. Hey, Cassidy and Sundance. Can you really trust these guys?"

"Of course, otherwise I wouldn't have come here, but we can't stay too long, plus we may need to get rid of the car in case there is a tracking device on it."

The plan was hatched. Jane knew nearly everyone in the area. The good, bad and indifferent and Joe knew she could arrange for the car to disappear. That left them stranded for transport, but maybe travelling around using public transport was a safer option.

An hour passed and Jane returned with Julia looking so much better after a shower and change of clothes.

"How you feeling now?" Joe asked.

"Feeling much better. Thank you, Jane."

"Ok. Right you lot, sit yourselves down, I'll put on some breakfast" Jane instructed.

The smell of cooked sausages and bacon was a welcome reminder of what life used to be like for them all. Smell is such an ordinary sensation that everyone takes for granted. *'How quick life can change'* Joe thought as he sat pondering about the events of the last few weeks.

After breakfast Caelan nodded to Joe to meet him outside. Jane and Julia remained in the kitchen, and Julia was enjoying chatting to someone who was genuinely lovely and did not judge. They got on well.

"What's up?"

"I don't know. It seems odd just sitting there as if nothing has happened."

"I think we need it to get our heads around what's happened and to re-group our thoughts. Jane knows by the way and she's fine with everything, but the boys don't."

"We can't keep running forever, Joe."

"I know mate. We just need to think."

They sat chatting and going through various scenarios and options for what seemed an eternity.

"So we're agreed then?" Caelan asked after some time.

"Yes. I'll speak to Jane later and get it sorted if she agrees. I have to say I like the idea."

For the remainder of the day Julia seemed to be getting better, becoming more herself than the shell-shocked woman she had been since she was separated from Mike. Joe kept looking at her as she sat there, chatting away with the sunlight shining through the kitchen window onto her beautiful face.

'God, I love you' Joe thought as he was still in disbelief that they were together. He only wished it could have been in different, and normal, circumstances.

That night Simon returned home with the boys and as usual, Jane had their meals waiting. Afterwards he left and re-entered carrying a crate of beer and a bag with wine bottles clinking.

"I thought we could catch-up" Simon said as he tore open the cardboard crate and handed out the beer.

They sat there discussing everything but nothing, and kept away from what had happened. Simon and the boys were unaware of the secret that was being kept from them.

Joe couldn't sleep as he lay next to Julia on the sofa, his arm gently wrapped around her, feeling her chest moving against him as she slept. He just wanted to stay there forever. He listened to the noises the night brought to a rural farm, and it seemed as though the noises were talking to him as he tuned in to each creak of a branch, the screech of an owl or the wind racing down the open fire chimney. He fell asleep thinking about Julia.

THE EDITOR

"Hello, is that the news desk?" Jane asked.

"That is correct you have got through to the Daily News. How can we help?" the female voice said.

Jane went on to explain that she needed to speak with the Editor and gave the very basic details of the reasons. She was put through almost immediately.

The Editor answered in a very uninterested voice and Jane found herself repeating the previous discussion. The Editor went quiet. His own newspaper, along with every other national or local paper, covered the story of Joe 'attempting to blow up the Prime Minister' then the shooting in the hospital. It was one of those rare stories that they would all fight for to get an exclusive interview.

"Hang on a second."

Although it was obvious he tried to cover up the phone with his hand, she could hear his shouting.

"Get me the fucking CEO now, I don't care if he is in a meeting drag him out and get him down here NOW!"

He returned to talk to Jane.

"OK. I just need to discuss a couple of things with my boss and I will call you back. So to summarise, you know where they are, and exactly what has happened and they are willing to talk to us?"

"That is right, but you will need to come alone and any sign of the police or anyone else and you won't get to meet them."

"OK I'll call you back."

Jane had used the pay as you go phone Joe had given her so as not to be traced. They waited for the call back.

Eventually the phone vibrated and Jane picked up the call, but did not answer.

"Is that you Jane? This is James O'Brian the Editor."

"Hi, yes this is Jane."

"OK, we are good to go, but can we meet today?"

He asked knowing he had little time before the hot story lost its appeal to his readers.

Being that they were a national newspaper and their head office was in London, Jane knew it would take him some time to get there, but nonetheless agreed and gave him the details Joe had written down for her. The meet was to take place some fifteen miles away in an abandoned barn which had once belonged to Jane's father.

"OK, so 4pm. I'll be there" he said and hung up the phone.

Joe and Caelan had been writing frantically to get their plan on paper and handed it to Jane.

"What do you think?"

"Well it certainly puts the point across."

"Are you sure you're OK with this?" Joe asked before throwing the page from the pad into the open fire.

"Of course, if it helps you all, then no bother."

They only had a few hours to prepare as she gave them the exact location of the barn.

"Baby, we will need to go there well before Jane arrives to ensure we know he hasn't been followed. I would prefer it if you stayed here. It's safe, and you can relax but if you want to come along with us, that's OK too."

"I don't want to be away from you again."

The car pulled out of the farm with the three of them heading to the meeting point with all of the weapons and ammunition checked; they were ready to stake out the location.

They arrived some forty minutes later as the single track led them to an isolated and sheltered barn made of crumbling, red bricks and an asbestos roof which had seen better days.

They parked the car some feet away from the barn and walked around looking at various vantage points. The car could be parked back on the main road in a lay-by as the agreed rendezvous point, and as the ground was dry there would be no signs of their vehicle being there first.

Joe pointed out a safe location for himself and Julia, and another potential ambush position for Caelan if needed; he would be ready too if things went wrong.

At least two hours before the agreed meeting time the vehicle had been moved and they too were in place.

"Julia, I need you to promise me something. If this goes terribly wrong or you get scared, get back to the car using the path behind us and drive back to Simon and Jane's. Stay there until we get back."

It was more of an instruction than a request.

"Please tell me everything will be OK, Joe?" she asked nervously. "It will all be fine."

He was lying of course and deep inside him he was unsure of what was going to happen, who would turn up or how the day would pan out. Inside he was frightened. This time, not only was he fighting for his life but for the future of them all, and for justice.

The wind could be heard blowing gently against the top of the trees, combined with the chorus of various bird songs and the lush green foliage rustling, Joe closed his eyes and remembered what it was like to be at one with mother-nature.

He had always loved being outdoors, from rock climbing to running and from survival courses to camping. His being at one with the environment soon came to a halt when he heard the over-revving of a car engine.

A small, red, saloon car appeared in the distance and Jane's face could be seen in the afternoon sun, shining through the windscreen.

Jane, as planned, parked immediately next to the barn and remained in the car. She looked calm and gave nothing away that they were nearby in the undergrowth.

Caelan was only a few yards away from Jane's car. She was one of life's true gems who everyone loved and Caelan could only just resist the temptation to wave to her, but he knew he had to remain in his covert hide. He also knew he didn't know what may follow, and he had to keep his surveillance position without compromising himself and those around him.

Julia knew she had to remain silent. After all, she had been used to it in her marriage, always there but remaining silent unless having to agree with Mike.

"Joe, I just want to say that whatever happens, know that I truly love you." Joe was surprised at the sudden comment and turned to look at her.

"Baby, I seriously love you. I will always make sure you never have the life you had before."

He gently touched her face as she hugged and kissed him on his cheek knowing he would only do what was best for her, for them both.

It wasn't long before a second vehicle could be heard in the distance coming down the track. It was at this point in time that that both Joe and Caelan needed to step up their game, as they moved deeper into the mental operational mode.

The shotguns Jane had sneaked out of the house now allowed them to train the weapons on any potential targets heading towards them. Joe also knew, due to his training, he needed to do something more than to concentrate on the main contact who may be acting as a decoy for any other potential assailants.

He whispered to Julia to stay low and not to move as he went to move further away around the perimeter of the barn. It was a common tactic of the military to ensure that the primary target did not have another team covering them, since their first reconnaissance some two hours earlier.

Joe could not find any indications of unwanted attention or presence and he moved back to his original position. Julia had curled up into the foetal position waiting for Joe to return. He touched her gently on the shoulder, and slid next to her into his fire position as the black, four-wheel drive, executive car approached Jane's position.

The lone driver was mid 40's, white with slick, black hair wearing aviator style sunglasses, a suit and open-necked blue shirt. His posture and driving indicated he was not aware he was being followed or accompanied, and both of them watched him as he approached. Jane immediately recognised him from his pictures they had looked at on the internet that morning.

The Lexus came to a halt next to Jane's car and O'Brian opened the driver's door and stepped towards the red car. He opened the passenger door and climbed inside to meet Jane, and he looked uncomfortable as his tall figure leaned forward to fit into the small saloon.

"Jane?" he asked as he held out his hand to shake hers.

"James, yes I am Jane."

"OK, so where are they?"

Jane had rehearsed in her own mind time and time again what Joe had told her.

"Don't worry they are nearby. They want to make sure you're not being followed. We can wait for them to tell us it's all OK."

"I told you I would come on my own." He was surprised at their caution of him.

They sat there in silence until Joe moved from his position keeping the cars in-between him and his guest. He knelt down to the side of O'Brian's car, took out the pistol, slipped off the safety catch and placed it behind his back, then stood up and walked around to allow himself to be visible to them both.

"You can get out now" Jane instructed him.

He left the confines of her car and stood in front of Joe as Jane put the car into gear and drove off as instructed.

"Joe Forrester?"

"Thank you for coming and sorry about the secrecy, but I am sure you can understand why?"

Joe pointed to the entrance to the barn for them to enter and explained to O'Brian what exactly had happened, from the start of him overhearing the conversation, to the shooting of the police officers in the hospital, as well as the disappearance of Ryan and the shooting of Gaby.

It was a lot for him to take in but O'Brian sat there trying to scribble everything down, as well as genuinely appearing to be shocked at each twist of events. Joe went on to explain that he suspected that the planners were now after them, that he feared for their lives, and how he would like to recruit the help of his paper to try to track Ryan down, as he was the only one that knew the truth, as well as tell their story to the nation to prove their innocence of all the speculation hitting the headlines.

"We can definitely help. How about we put you up in a secure location and arrange a proper interview. We can protect you?"

"It would be interesting to know how you would plan on doing that considering the police, with all their resources, failed to do exactly that!"

"OK, good point."

O'Brian realised what little impact the protection he could offer would be to them all.

Joe was asked some further details and he could see the shorthand notes of the Editor, which he couldn't decipher but he hoped it was word for word what he had said. He had never really trusted the media to portray the truth and not put their own, or a political, spin on things but he had no choice. He had fast run out of options, but at least the paper could target the nation to tell the people his version of events, and to try to at least get them the protection they desperately needed against the terrorists.

O'Brian shook Joe's hand and gave him his pledge to help him, but in return he wanted Joe's assurance that he would not approach any other media organisation. It was something that Joe was happy to agree with, after all there were few people they could trust. Both men stood and headed back to the car.

THE CHASE

"Did you really think I would have been followed?" O'Brian asked.

Before Joe could respond, the high caliber round shattered O'Brian's shoulder blade and sent him flying towards Joe. He hit the ground as Joe side-stepped him to duck behind the car.

"Caelan, get Julia and head back!"

Caelan ran from his cover aiming the shotgun in the direction of the unknown shooter to run towards Julia.

Joe picked up O'Brian, who was still conscious and bundled him into the passenger seat of his own car slumping forward in pain. Joe knew he needed help urgently.

He moved into the driver's seat, put the car into gear and reversed away from the barn. As he did so, he heard the second round hit the bodywork on his side. The third shot shattered the rear windscreen as it continued forward to shatter the front windscreen also. He took the pistol grip of his weapon and cleared the window of any further glass fragments giving him the visibility he needed to drive at speed down the lane towards the main road.

Joe kept trying to pull O'Brian back into the seat, but he was losing blood and leaning forward seemed a natural body reaction to such a shot. As he drove straight onto the main road, he only just missed oncoming vehicles as he skidded across the lane to head in the direction of the farm.

He passed by the lay-by and noticed the car which Julia and Caelan had been told to take back had already gone. Joe hoped they got away OK as he drove away from the shooter's position. He watched the rear view mirror constantly to ensure he wasn't being followed.

It was the two dark cars that he noticed overtaking the other vehicles, as well as nearly hitting the oncoming traffic having to swerve to miss them behind him, that alerted Joe to their vehicle being followed.

"Shit!" he shouted.

He couldn't risk overtaking the cars in front to get away, it was too dangerous and Joe wasn't the most experienced of drivers. The cars were getting nearer and Joe knew he had to do something to shake them.

The turning coming up on the right seemed to wind down towards a small village across the flat fields. He braked hard, ensuring the cars behind slammed on their brakes to slow the pursuing cars. He then accelerated hard in reverse to hit the car immediately behind. He sped off and turned down the side lane.

He didn't know where he was going or where it led, but he needed that space between him and the two chasing vehicles.

The village seemed to have no pedestrians or vehicles driving through, which was a bonus considering the speed Joe was going. He pulled into the driveway of a large house hoping the tall conifers would hide the car. He checked O'Brian again, who was looking very pale, but was still just conscious.

"Stay with me" he said, but only got a grunt of a response.

Joe heard the two cars speed past his location. He gave them a few seconds to get around the corner before pulling back out and heading back in the direction he had come from. Joe turned back onto the main road and continued towards the farm.

He was unaware that the lane he had just been driving on only went through the village, and joined the main road about a mile further up towards where he was travelling. He saw the two cars waiting to pull out from the junction in front and grabbed the Glock. He started shooting through the shattered window in their direction.

His first three shots hit the driver who was also surprised to have seen the car they were chasing and lost. The shots killed him outright, and his remaining rounds hit the male passenger and he seemed to slump side-wards, hitting his head on the side window.

The rear car had been untouched and tried to get around the static front car as Joe and O'Brian sped past. It wasn't long before the car was catching up. Joe seriously needed to think a different tactic to lose this one too.

He could see there were two occupants as the car was again aggressively overtaking to get nearer to their target. Joe was worried that they would soon be coming up to the turn-off towards the farm. He couldn't compromise their location as he passed by the turning to continue along the road. He didn't know where he was heading or how far the road continued, but a further two miles along he saw a sign for a roundabout.

He hit the roundabout hard, cutting up vehicles already turning to get an advantage from the pursuing car, and he noticed in his mirror that the car had been trapped behind the stationary vehicles which gave him the perfect opportunity to lose it.

He took a couple of further turnings keeping his bearings and parked up. He left the car and stood behind a tree on the opposite side of the road. He knew there were not that many turnings he could have taken after the roundabout, and he knew those following would soon catch them up. He waited for the car to make an appearance.

It wasn't long before the hostile car passed slowly at the end of the road and stopped. It reversed and entered the road driving slowly towards the damaged car. It stopped by the side and, before the passengers could exit, Joe ran across the road and shot the driver through the back of the head as he was looking at O'Brian's car.

The passenger was covered in his colleague's blood and brains. He turned in shock and went to grab his weapon, but never reached it as he was shot through the eye socket and slumped backwards.

Joe headed back with O'Brian towards the farm and could hear sirens in the background. As he pulled into the large barn, he noticed both Jane's and the stolen vehicle had been parked up, hopefully indicating that they had all got back OK.

He entered the kitchen with O'Brian being supported by his arm, but was met from the back of the door with the cold metal of a shotgun barrel. He froze for a minute until he heard Caelan's voice.

"Thank God your back."

O'Brian was placed on the large kitchen table with the help of Jane and Julia.

"What happened to him?" Jane asked.

Joe told them what had happened as they sat there in shock.

"Are you injured Joe?" Julia said as she approached him and touched his chest.

Joe looked down at his shirt and could see the large patch of blood that had come from O'Brian. There was a look of relief from Julia as she gave him a hug and held him tight. Joe could feel the love she had for him and kissed her passionately.

Jane attended to O'Brian's wounds.

"We need to get a doctor to deal with these properly."

"We can't, they will know it's a bullet wound and, they are obliged to inform the police."

"Good point. I know a vet who may help us" she said.

"A Vet? He's not a cow" Caelan joked.

"Can you trust him?"

"He's my cousin and yes, he's helped us before." Jane made the call.

O'Brian was getting worse as time went by and although Joe's combat medical training initially helped, it was limited due to the lack of equipment for stemming the blood and making him comfortable. He wished he had his military trauma kit with him, at least he could of stopped the bleeding and given him pain relief. They needed him to survive to tell their story.

It took just under an hour for Jane's cousin to arrive. The knock on the door surprised them all and hands went towards the weapons again. The door flung open and a stocky, blonde, middle-aged man entered.

"Right who needs their hooves cleaned?" He said as Jane grabbed his arm and showed him the damage the bullet had done.

He looked with surprise at the bullet wound. "Oh, OK, wasn't expecting this."

"Can you help, Dave?" Jane asked.

"Of course I can, it's only a bullet wound. I have to shove my arm up a cow's arse for a living, so digging around this pin-hole isn't an issue." Jane ran around him as he worked whilst the remainder sat around watching. Julia was washing the dishes and pottering around the kitchen making tea for everyone. It was her way of taking her mind of everything she had been a part of over the last few days. Her life with Mike seemed a lifetime ago as she now entered the world of a fugitive.

After an hour, Dave snapped off his surgical gloves, "Right, the good news is that he's going to be fine, well kind of. He needs to sleep for a few days, but his shoulder blade has had it and he will eventually need proper medical attention. The bad news is that he will never be able to have any more calves. Only kidding!"

No one in the room appreciated his weird, medical, slapstick comedy style, which was more in keeping with Blazing Saddles than a farmhouse in the middle of Nottinghamshire.

Dave left as quickly as he had arrived giving a simple wave as he drove off.

O'Brian was asleep due to the cocktail of animal injections he had received which is what he needed. At least they were dealing with an injury rather than a corpse Joe thought.

As he slept, the rest sat around discussing what they would tell Simon and the boys when they returned.

"How about we mistook him for a rabbit and shot him for dinner?" Caelan said as everyone just looked at him.

"OK, not a good idea. Sorry."

Jane rang Simon and asked him to get the boys to stay at their grandmother's that evening.

By the time Simon had returned it had been agreed to tell him the truth. He was a large man and would probably go mad after finding out Jane's involvement in the day's events, but with a body lying on the dining table they had no choice. Surprisingly, Simon didn't express any emotion apart from making sure his wife was OK.

"I know you think I don't know what's happening Joe, and although I'm just a farmer, I do know everything. We're here for you and will do what we can to help."

Jane looked on in shock. She had not told him, nor had he let on before, she didn't know he knew. Joe shook his hand.

"Thanks, Simon, that means a lot."

Simon seemed to take control as he ordered O'Brian to be carried through to the living room and placed on the sofa. He then asked if anyone else knew they were there as well as what cars had been brought onto the farm. He got all of the answers he needed and asked them if they wanted to get rid of the cars.

They all agreed that dumping the cars, apart from O'Brian's, was a good idea and Simon left again. A tractor could be heard in the distance and Joe knew the farm was big enough to be able to hide a few cars in one of the many sheds, hangers and barns, and after some time, Simon returned.

"Right, beers all round" he said as he again went to the fridge and handed everyone a drink.

"What are your plans, Joe?"

"That is a good question, I didn't expect for him to be shot for starters" Joe said as he pointed towards the living room.

"I suppose we are limited to what we can do. On one hand, we should be able to hand ourselves in to the police, but how do we know we can trust them? On the other hand it would be good just to disappear, but the planners seem to know where we are every time we have a plan."

"Right, give me all the devices you have, phones, iPad whatever..."

"Why, do you need to make a call?" Caelan said jokingly as Simon stood up and leaned on the table in front of him.

"Listen to me, the cars, phones, laptops and all other technical pieces of equipment can be traced, so either hand them over or get out."

He was a hulk of a man and not to be messed with and the anger in his voice was a reminder to them all of how serious their situation was.

Simon took all the devices and placed them in the microwave for a few seconds.

"That will fry the phones."

"Where did you learn that?" Jane asked.

"On TV."

Everyone looked around not believing him and wondered where he really had learnt that trick.

The discussion revolved around agreeing their next move and what the best plan of action was for them all.

"Look, let's get some sleep and we can think about this tomorrow" Simon said.

Joe and Caelan went for a walk around the farm just to check on any unwanted movement.

The night was cold and the clear sky gave the light needed to see. After their previous recce, they didn't want to take for granted they were alone. Caelan wanted to make sure of their safety.

"Should we take shifts staying up all night?"

"I think so, I'll take the first stag."

They agreed the best position was opposite the main house inside a small barn that acted as a store room for various pieces of machinery.

"Can I come with you?" Julia asked when Joe had told them what they were doing.

"You need to sleep baby, I'll only be across there and only for a few hours then I'll come and join you."

She looked sad, but knew he was right, she was still tired and needed to have a clear head to be able to help them all, and also herself, over the course of the next few days, or would it be weeks? None of them knew what was in store.

Caelan relieved Joe just before 2am.

"All OK and nothing to report, it's been as quiet as a mouse."

"Good. Go and get some rest."

Caelan tapped him on the arm and left him to be at one with the night.

THE FARM

D aylight started coming through the window as Jane lay there. She felt the heat of the early morning sun on her face and she stirred before the memory of the previous day kicked in. She sat up and put on her dressing gown and headed down stairs.

Joe and Julia were already making tea and coffee for everyone when she entered the room.

Joe left Julia and Jane chatting in the kitchen and headed over to Caelan with his welcomed hot drink.

"Morning mate, is everything OK?"

"The only thing was Simon leaving for work at five this morning. Oh and cow's shit stinks worse than army food."

"I always thought you should spend more time outdoors and get a real life."

They joked as they started to make their way back to the kitchen. Joe had already checked on O'Brian before supplying the coffee to Caelan, but he was still asleep and he knew he should try to wake him soon.

The coffee tasted strong, but it was welcome and made them both more alert. Before they entered the house Caelan stopped.

"Joe, what's the plan, mate, we can't stay here forever?"

"I don't know. I am pretty worried someone in the police may have compromised us and leaked the details to the planners, so we can't trust anyone outside of those that are here now."

They agreed to ask Jane for her thoughts; after all she had been both a tower of strength as well as level-headed throughout their short stay so far.

Julia was, as always busying herself around the kitchen chatting to Jane when they entered.

"Morning boys" Jane said in an almost Bette Midler manner.

It was the first time Caelan had noticed Jane's figure and he smiled at her. Jane was a confident and buxom woman who had seen and experienced a million Caelan's throughout her life. More importantly, she knew how to handle them.

"Jane, we really need to talk about what we should do. I really don't want to put you guys at any further risk" Joe stated.

"Simon and I have talked about this and we are agreed you should stay here for a while, after all it's either here or the Village Hall."

Joe smiled as he remembered with warmth the small, old, church hall where he had been a guest on many occasions. It was a place where the locals met regularly, not just for the cheap alcohol, but it was run by them and they therefore had a vested interest in making it socially and economically viable.

Jane went on to state that her boys were staying at one of their friends for a while.

"The bedrooms are all sorted, I have changed the sheets and Caelan you're in Will's room at the back, and Julia, you and Joe are in Sam's room. At least we can try to get some sleep."

Joe looked at Caelan as if to say *'that really isn't going to happen.'*

"Thanks Jane. You're a star as always."

He liked the idea of sharing a bed night after night with Julia, but he was worried about Caelan disappearing again.

"You OK staying, pal?"

"God, yes I am. I was brought up on a farm. This takes me back to a place I miss. Anyway, we're now in this together."

Later that morning O'Brian started to come around from his drug induced sleep.

"James, can you hear me?"

Jane's voice got louder as he started to come around whilst she was tending his dressings. His blurred vision, combined with the pain made him groan loudly.

"Lay still, you will be OK."

"Where am I?"

"You're safe, that's all that matters."

Jane chatted to him for some time as she changed his dressing and explained what had happened and how he was lucky to be alive. She also told him that they had to hide at the farm until it was safe to leave.

"They told me everything would be OK."

Jane immediately left the room and explained to Joe what O'Brian had just said.

"What have you done?" Joe said with anger in his voice.

O'Brian explained that he had a responsibility to his boss to tell him what story he was chasing, as it was unusual that an Editor would take on this role directly. He also explained that he had to give all relevant details of who the contact was, the location and the general benefit to the company. In this case it was the potential one-off chance to interview a police suspect of planning and carrying out a terrorist attack, as well as killing two police officers. He also explained that his boss had a responsibility to inform the police of the details, otherwise they could liable to prosecution for withholding information under the Terrorism Act.

Joe sat down and couldn't believe that yet again they had been deceived. *'Was there anyone he could trust'* he thought to himself as he left the room after asking to speak with Simon and Jane outside.

"We're in deep shit. O'Brian, or one of his media idiots have told the authorities where he was heading and who he was speaking to. It's only a matter of time before they put two and two together. You all need to leave now."

"Not a chance. We don't leave mates to deal with things on their own" Jane said.

"The only person that can help us is Ryan, and we think he's dead. Unless we can get hold of him, we're stuffed."

"Let me try" Jane said.

"The last person that did that got shot."

Joe thought about Gaby and her fate at the hands of her attackers and couldn't risk that happening to anyone else.

Jane touched him on his arm.

"Please let me try Joe. We know someone high up in the police and she is a good friend. We can trust her."

She walked off and Simon tapped Joe on the arm. "If anyone can track him down, it's her."

Later that day Simon asked to speak to both Joe and Caelan. "Jane and I are going to leave you guys here for a few days. We need to get away to give you some space and to allow us to think about everything that's happened over the last few days. This is not up for discussion, Joe; this is what we are going to do, what we need to do. You will all be OK. Trust me! Here are the keys to the jeep. It's parked at the other end of the field where the summerhouse is."

Joe understood their need to escape but knew you couldn't argue with either of them once they had set their minds to do something. He also felt guilty that they felt the need to leave their own home and had risked everything for him. Joe went inside as he watched them go in their car. Joe felt sad, but at the same time happy as his two friends drove away to safety.

"Guys, I need to talk to you" Joe said as he entered the living room to Julia and Caelan.

"What is it, Joe?" Julia said.

"Simon and Jane have left as it is unsafe for them to be here anymore. I need to ask you both to leave too. Here are the keys to a jeep at the end of the field. Please go and head to anywhere as far away from here as you can."

There was no need to think as both of them gave their response one after the other.

"No chance pal. I'm not leaving you."

"Joe, I love you and I am not going to abandon you, my sweetheart." Joe, for the first time in his life, felt true happiness. He had a true love and a true friend, yet he knew he needed to set them free from his own incarceration and the self-destruct path he seemed to have travelled down.

He tried to plead with them. "Please, get out of here." They both refused to leave.

Joe explained what O'Brian had told them in the hope that this would change their mind.

"How about we pin him to a tree naked and tell the media he is there?" Caelan asked.

"Funny you should say. I think we should get O'Brian to a hospital soon to ensure our story is told."

It was agreed after some debate that Caelan would take O'Brian to a city hospital, and then make a call to one of their competitor newspapers explaining what had happened.

Joe knew he only had limited time before the authorities or the planners arrived, and needed to get everyone away from the area but Julia still refused to leave his side, knowing what the potential consequences may be. The true love they had for each other was shining through as Julia still refused to leave him.

After Caelan and O'Brian had left under the cover of early nightfall and across country, Joe could hear the distant noise of police sirens and turned to Julia.

"Baby, please know that I love you and I am sorry for everything. I wish things could have been different."

"I love you too, my baby, and I'm here with you no matter what."

Joe felt a true sense of guilt that their love had led to a potential shootout with the planners or a potential stand-off with the authorities. He hugged her and told her he loved her again. He really couldn't tell her enough how he felt.

The familiar sirens of the emergency services were getting louder and Joe knew that they were heading towards them at speed. Eventually he could see the distant, blue lights flickering over the rolling countryside. He checked his weapons and ammunition and placed them at strategic locations around the kitchen, which gave them the best protection as the walls were overly thick in places.

He had planned for a shoot-out so many times before when training for Iraq and Afghanistan, from setting a simple shotgun against a door as a booby trap, to home-made explosives against the windows.

Julia just sat there watching him knowing how much she truly loved him. Knowing she would die for him, to be with him till the end having no thoughts about Mike or her past life.

The sirens were closer and it was only a matter of minutes before they arrived at the farm.

"Joe, I know they will be here soon, but I have to ask. Are you sure you have not done anything wrong?"

Joe's heart was ripped apart as he couldn't believe she had asked him that. He felt betrayed for that split second by the only woman he had ever loved.

"I swear on your life, that I have done nothing wrong. All I did was to overhear the planners discuss a terrorist attack and try to alert the authorities. That's it."

Julia stood up and held him like never before.

"I love you so, so much and whatever you want me to do, just ask Joe."

He looked into her eyes and knew she meant it and he could sense she knew this was the end for them both, but the tears in her eyes gave away how scared she was.

"Everything will be fine, baby, you watch. Have faith."

As the vehicles entered the farm, the sirens fell silent. They fanned out to form a display of blue lights across the buildings as they pulled up in front and to the rear of the main house. Joe could see through the lace curtains that the Armed Response Unit had taken up strategic positions, whilst the specialist search teams were making their way to the outhouses surrounding the farmyard. It was standard operating procedure to secure the exterior first.

He knew they would cover every possibility of an escape route, and after what he had experienced so far, he knew he couldn't trust them to keep them safe or even from passing their details to the planners.

Surely they had to have people on the inside; there could be no other explanation for what had happened to his sister, Ryan and the armed guards at the hospital. It was all just too convenient to be coincidence.

Joe knew they would prefer him, and anyone associated, be killed rather than be taken alive. At least that way they wouldn't be able to tell anyone about what had happened. No answers to any awkward questions.

He had to protect his one, true love, even if that meant giving up his own life, but how? He knew he couldn't trust those on the outside, nor could he force her to leave. It crossed his mind that she was in exactly the same boat as he was right now, with nowhere to go back to, nowhere to stay and nowhere to run.

He checked the magazine of the pistol again and took the top two rounds out and placed them in his pocket. He knew that if all else failed, he could make the decision for him and Julia to finally be together in death if there was no other way. He would rather do it himself than be left to the fate of the attackers.

Joe's heart was racing as the adrenalin began to pump around his body. Julia was also nervous and it showed in her face. Joe took her hand and led her to the far corner of the kitchen next to the Aga and placed her on the floor.

"Baby, please stay right here."

He knew the cast iron oven would give her the best protection from any flying glass, stray bullets or whatever else they threw or aimed their way.

"Right we have the Tactical Firearms Unit in position and we have a one mile cordon set up" said the Tactical Group Leader to the Incident Commander outside of the farm house.

Superintendent Evans had served in the police for over thirty years, and had been the nearest senior officer available after getting the call from someone calling themselves Ryan from Scotland Yard. His remit was to secure the location ensuring those inside remained there at all costs thus preventing another major UK terrorist attack, larger than any other witnessed in the history of modern warfare. He was also told that he was not to allow any information to be passed onto to any other rank and file officer. It was a strictly closed-door, top secret operation.

Evans was familiar with being kept in the dark, even at his senior level; further up the ladder, the worse the politics! After calling Ryan and briefing him on the situation, he was told to pull back all but essential officers to the outer cordon at the entrance road to the farm and await his attendance. Despite this being against police procedure for such a stand-off, Evans did what he was instructed and sat in his unmarked car awaiting Ryan's attendance.

Joe wanted to pace across the kitchen floor, but he knew marksmen would be ready to take the shot if the chance arose if they had been given permission. He sat next to Julia knowing that at some point, they would either hear from them, or they would come crashing through the door or windows at any time.

Joe placed his arm around her shoulders and placed her head on his chest.

"No matter what happens, baby, please know that I love you with all of my heart."

"I love you too Joe. At least we're together."

Joe thought about the two bullets he had in his pocket and knew time was not on their side.

The phone rang again.

"This is Superintendent Evans speaking."

"We have just come through the cordon and I need you to pull back every remaining officer from the scene to the exterior cordon."

"I'm sorry. Who is this?"

"Ryan, I spoke to you earlier. Do what I have asked right now or I'll have you demoted and back on road duty within the hour."

Evans cut the call short and over the police radio network he ordered everyone back as instructed.

'This isn't right' he thought to himself as he waited for the three vehicles making their way to him.

The unmarked cars stopped short of the yard and a lone figure walked towards Evans.

"Ryan?"

"Yes, that is me."

He raised the pistol and shot Evans through the windpipe.

Evans clutched at his throat trying to breathe and stop the spurting blood as the second shot entered his chest. He fell backwards to the floor never knowing why he had been killed.

Joe had jumped to his feet after hearing the shots and had placed himself at the side of the small window.

"Fuck, they have shot one of their own."

He knew the planners had got people on the inside, but didn't think they would go to this level, or have enough power to override the police he thought as he ran over to Julia.

"We have to go now."

"Where can we go Joe?"

He didn't know. He only knew they couldn't stay there it would mean certain death.

He had the pistol in his hand and poised ready for an attack, yet everything was surprisingly quiet. He placed Julia back on the floor and lifted his finger to her lips. He had no choice now. No other way out.

"Shush, baby. Don't say anything and close your eyes." He slowly lifted the pistol towards her head.

The sharp creaking coming from one of the wooden panels on the wall opposite made Joe spin around and aim the pistol away from Julia. He knelt there in the aiming position as the wall seemed to come away from itself.

It was almost a psychedelic moment and he had to shake his head in disbelief as a large figure emerged.

"Joe, it's me, George. Don't shoot" the dark figure said.

Joe didn't know if to release the whole magazine into him at first, but it took a couple of seconds to recognise his old friend's voice.

"What the fuck are you doing here?"

"No time for that, come with me, Simon and Jane showed me the way, see there really is a secret tunnel. They are waiting in the truck. Come on, man, get a move on."

Still in a state of shock, Joe grabbed Julia's hand and led her towards the wall; he had always trusted George and had no reason to disbelieve him now.

Joe couldn't believe not only had there really been a secret tunnel after all, but that George had appeared out of nowhere. Then again, he always did say he had seen the tunnels during some of Simon's ramblings.

The thick double-panelled wall closed behind sealing them off from their potential attackers.

As they moved through the tunnel at speed with only George's torch as a guide, they could hear the smashing of glass back in the farmhouse as those waiting outside started their assault.

They moved faster along the stone-walled tunnel with darkness in front of them and sure death behind them.

After what seemed like an eternity, and passing various alternative turnings, George knelt down and turned towards them.

"Right, we're about to go outside. Simon is waiting with a shotgun so keep your bloody voices down."

George moved the large slab of stone from the tunnel "Simon, it's me, George, I have them both with me!"

Joe knew something wasn't right by what George had said and how he had said it. George was an experiences soldier like himself, and he had never heard him so scared. Joe tapped George on the shoulder.

"I'm sorry, Joe" George said with pure sadness in his voice.

Joe knew what was coming and punched George so hard his jaw snapped as he fell to the floor in sheer agony.

He grabbed the torch and quickly replaced the stone to cover up the hole and handed Julia the torch.

"Take the first tunnel on the left, turn out the torch, crouch down and wait for me there."

Julia disappeared into the darkness and Joe knew it wouldn't be long before they entered the tunnel.

The stone moved again and a torch was seen shining in the entrance. Joe hit the hand with the butt of the pistol and grabbed the torch. He started shooting at the lights outside watching, them fall as he could hear and feel bullets hitting the stones around him. He ran back along the tunnel to Julia.

Joe found her sitting there in a ball. "Baby, come on we have to move."

He grabbed her again and ran down the secondary tunnel where she had been waiting.

He didn't know where it led, if anywhere at all, but all he knew was that he had to make good speed to get away from both sets of attackers.

The tunnel turned in various directions and he felt disoriented until finally they came across a stone wall directly in front of them. He turned off the torch and looked up.

There was a grill about three feet above them. It was big enough to get them through but he needed to try to move it first. It was stiff with age but eventually he managed to prise it out of its housing.

He stopped for a few seconds to listen to the noises both in the tunnel and above ground. He could hear the voices of those already following them underground, but nothing above. He jumped and grabbed the side of the hole and peered into the night.

He looked around and could only see darkness as he pulled himself up and clambered out of the hole. Once he knew it was clear, he leaned down and pulled up Julia.

He replaced the grill once they were free from the dark tunnel, and placed some foliage over it to fool the attackers into believing it had not been moved for a long time. They ran towards the nearest hedgerow.

He couldn't initially make out where he was, but he could just see the power station cooling towers in the background of the darkened sky.

He knew Simon and Jane would not have betrayed them, and hoped they were OK. The only place he could think of heading towards, and that he knew, was the local village hall some two miles away. He remembered the layout as he had been there many times when Simon and Jane were either drinking in there or helping behind the bar.

They ran as fast as they could, occasionally taking breaks for Julia to catch her breath. On entering the village, Joe made sure they kept in the shadows of the overhanging trees that lined the small lanes to keep away from potential prying eyes.

The fence at the back of the hall had always been loose and security was never an issue in such rural locations. Joe moved the panel to one side allowing Julia through to the garden of the hall, which was a small seated area, but at least it was under cover and it was dark and quiet.

He knew from when he had been there on previous occasions no one had ever opened up before 11am. They had a few hours to rest before thinking their next move, whatever that may be.

Joe couldn't sleep and he couldn't help thinking that he was almost about to end it all for them both when he thought salvation had arrived. They had been tricked again by someone who had been his best friend for so long. Maybe he had been forced to do it? That could be the only possible reason as George was a good man, a good friend and a trusted confidant.

He didn't know what to do next as he sat there cuddled up to Julia to keep her warm. With a few hours away from the attackers, he seriously needed to think what they were going to do and how he was going to protect Julia.

The night was cold, but at least they were safe for now.

Joe couldn't sleep and he eventually managed to prise open the rear door to the hall and led Julia inside, and behind the bar he poured a large brandy for Julia and himself.

"I think we need this."

They sat there looking at each other knowing things were going from bad to worse.

"We're safe here."

Julia looked up at him with pain in her eyes, and he knew he had put her through much more than she deserved and for the first time, he felt guilty about taking her away from Mike. Not for any other reason but her safety. She was better off in a volatile relationship than not to be alive.

The hour passed with very little said and Julia really looked tired. The phone behind the bar rang to their surprise and Joe looked at the clock.

It was 3am and who the hell would be ringing at this time of the night he thought. He also knew not to answer it, but it kept on ringing and ringing. He knew now that if he didn't answer at some point, the adjoining houses would hear it and become suspicious. The last thing he needed was for them to call the police, or to come looking themselves, he thought as he picked up the receiver.

"Joe if that's you, please listen to me. It's Jane. I took a chance and thought you may go there if things went wrong, it's the only place you ever felt comfortable around other people with us and away from our house. I have left an envelope for you under the counter. There is money and a set of keys in it. The keys are for the red car outside and to Dean and Angie's house as they are away at the moment. Do you remember where it is?"

"Yes I remember."

"Whatever you do, do not go anywhere else, it's not safe."

"My God Jane, are you guys OK?"

"Yes we're fine and at my brother's. Just stay safe and I will call you in a couple of days in the house. Everything you need is there."

"I told you it would be OK" Simon could be heard shouting in the background.

"Thank you so much, both of you, we owe you."

"Oh we will hold you to that I am sure."

She hung up the phone.

Joe noticed Julia looking at him with surprise that the call had been for him.

"Are we really safe here Joe?"

"Yes for now, but we have to move onto somewhere else, baby. It's not too far and we now have a legitimate car to use."

He told her everything Jane had said.

"So what happens when we get to the house, do we have to keep moving again and again?"

"We need to disorientate those chasing us and the more we move to begin with the better. The place is secure and we will be safe there until we can plan long term."

He had moved into military mode; Emotions removed and confidence replacing fear.

Julia nodded, and she knew he was right and would follow him to · the ends of the earth.

THERE IS ALWAYS ANOTHER WAY

The car started first time and they drove off hoping to distance themselves further from their attackers. The house had not changed since his last visit with it's stone-clad exterior and the rolling-style driveway gates electronically and automatically synchronised with their cars.

The gates started to slide open as the car approached, but Joe felt conscious that although they were still under the cover of night, someone may not recognise the occupants of the car and report them to the police. Then again, it was one of the most renowned estates in the county for its high crime rates, and stolen cars were a part of it's illegal black market activities.

The small car drove straight onto the small forecourt and the gates securely closed behind them, and as they did Joe reversed the car back to the gates to ensure that the car became a block so no other vehicle could enter if somehow the gates were manually operated.

They sat in the car for a few minutes to make sure there was no movement in or outside of the house. Joe checked his pistol again.

He entered the main door cautiously and disabled the alarm using the code Jane had supplied in the envelope. It was no surprise that it was the same year of Dean's regiment's formation which Joe knew all too well. The alarm gave the usual loud audible sound after he entered the numbers 1.6.5.0.

"The alarm system has successfully been disabled" it automatically announced.

Joe knew they were in one of the most secure homes in the county, but he still kept his hand on the pistol. He had learnt to be cautious of every situation in every environment, from the streets of Northern Ireland to the plains of Africa and everywhere in between.

Despite Jane telling him that they were away, Joe checked the house and was surprised how much food and drink there was in the cupboards and fridge. Jane had always been able to forward think and to judge other people's movements before they could, and that always surprised him. She was definitely in the wrong job!

Joe had always had a soft spot for Jane, for how she made him feel special every time they all met up. Her and her family, as well as their close friends, were without doubt people you can trust in times of need.

They were people you wanted to be around who made you forget any issues or problems you had. Once again they had all rallied around, and shown their friendship and love for Joe and two others they had never met before. Just like the first time George had met them and had felt the same way.

The house felt safe and secure from outside prying eyes, and it wasn't long before Julia was soaking in a well-needed hot bath with a glass of red wine. Joe sat on the edge of the bath watching her as she closed her eyes and sank deeper into the bubbles. It was the first time since making love to her in his room that he had noticed her true beauty and her wonderful naked body. He felt the need to hold her again.

He slipped into the bath with her and they sat looking into each other's eyes in the warmth of the water, knowing they were together to the end despite life's obvious alternative intentions.

What they had was true love, a love like no other, a love that is only found once in a lifetime, and they didn't care about how they had got to where they were and they both felt a need to feel each other again, to hold and embrace each other closer than ever before.

Joe woke the next morning first to the sound of heavy traffic passing through the estate and not, to his surprise, in his usual alarmed state.

It felt good being in a bed again as he lay there with his arms around the love of his life; something he had dreamed of doing for so long. He felt the need to stay there and not move as she lay there sleeping.

He could feel her heart beating against her breast and he wanted her again as he watched her sleeping and kissed her neck. Julia responded to his kiss and turned into him.

"Morning baby."

"I want you. I need you. I love you and I desire you. You make me feel amazing. You are such a beautiful, precious man, and a man that I truly love, my gorgeous sweetheart."

Joe was blown away, and he felt a tear roll down his cheek as he gulped a breath of air.

"My baby, that's so lovely. I love you with every breath I take, with every heart-beat I have. God, I love you."

They made love knowing true passion and why they had travelled the long and hard road to true love, and why they needed to be together. They forgot about the potential fate that they both faced as they felt the soft skin of each other. It was as if they were living two lives as fugitives being hunted down, and the other as long, lost, passionate lovers.

The morning seemed to drag by as they both sat around the house waiting for the phone to ring but it wasn't long before reality kicked in.

"What are we going to do now Joe?"

He knew that he had to lie to her, something he had always vowed not to do.

"Baby, we're going to be OK."

He knew deep down that they could never truly be safe from either the authorities or the planners, no matter where they went.

Joe started making lunch with Julia watching him, never wanting to be away from his side. He was keeping himself busy to try to stop thinking about what was going to happen in their on-the-run lives.

They sat at the table watching each other with both love and frustration of the situation in their eyes. The rest of the afternoon was spent waiting for the phone to ring and cuddling up on the sofa. They found a film channel on the TV, deliberately keeping away from the various news channels, and watched an old black and white film which took their minds away from the reality of their never-ending situation. It appeared as though they were an ordinary couple in an ordinary house in an ordinary city, but the reality of the situation was far from that. Nothing in their lives was, nor would ever be, normal again.

After waking in the early evening, Joe lay there with Julia in his arms and he knew he wanted to spoil Julia one more time, the way she had always deserved to be treated. The way he had always wanted to and the way he knew he couldn't going forward. He felt sad that he had failed her in life, and had moved her from a relatively stable environment to being chased across the country fighting for their lives.

He slipped from the sofa without waking her and again checked all of the doors and windows, then headed upstairs.

The water flowed as Joe sat on the edge of the bath trying to think fast about their next move. All the time he couldn't get Julia from his mind. He poured in some oil which, not only felt soft but, spread the wonderful aroma throughout the house.

He gently touched her soft warm face. "Wake up, my baby. I've run you a nice bath."

He led her by the hand into the candle-lit bathroom where he helped her get undressed. Each time he touched her, he wanted her so much, but he knew he couldn't this time.

Joe handed Julia the large glass of red wine and knelt next to the bath watching her.

"I want you to know, baby, that no matter what happens, I love you with all of my heart."

He leaned forward to meet her lips. "I love you too baby."

Joe left the room and returned downstairs with a heavy heart.

He knew there was only one way out of this situation, and one in which everyone around him could be free from this persecution.

The phone rang as he had finished cleaning the kitchen. "Joe, it's me, Jane. I hope you two are OK?"

"The police have now released the farm back to us after their crap attempt of repairing all of their damage. Do you want to come back here? We have just borrowed a caravan for you two and it's hidden in the deer woods on the hill. No one ever goes there. Caelan is now back here too."

Joe heard the smashing of the wine glass as it fell from Julia's hand. "Shit!" Joe shouted as he dropped the phone and ran upstairs to find Julia sitting up in the bath.

"I'm so sorry, Joe, I closed my eyes and accidently knocked it off of the side. I didn't even get to taste it."

Joe's heart was racing as he stood there with relief on his face. "That's OK. We need to go in a short time, baby."

He sat on the bed with his hands on his head *What the fuck was I thinking'* he said to himself knowing that he had laced the red wine with a cocktail of sleeping pills and headache tablets he had found in the bathroom cabinet to let Julia slip away in peace rather than let her continue going through this crap. He was then going to do the same himself.

'Thank God she smashed the glass' he thought as he slapped his head again and made a vow never to let her down again.

The drive back to the farm was a nervous one, but he knew the police would not be looking for the vehicle they were in. Just to make sure, he double backed on himself, every chance he could to be certain he wasn't being followed.

Eventually, he stopped just short of the farm entrance and waited for the next few cars to pass by before driving down to the house.

As they moved towards the front door, they were met by Caelan. "Oh, you're back are you?"

Jane was again pottering about the kitchen when they entered and she hugged them both in her usual, loving way.

"I've missed you both."

"Thank you. You are wonderful" Julia said as she gave her another genuine hug.

"What about me?" Simon said as he entered the room carrying a couple of bottles of wine and some beers.

"We'll I'm not hugging you!" Joe said.

Julia went up to him and hugged him, and gave him a kiss on the cheek. It was the first time Joe had ever seen him go bright red with embarrassment as they all burst out laughing.

It was the first time they had, since it all began, but deep down Joe would live with the guilt of the near miss with Julia and the red wine for the rest of his life, no matter how long that may be.

The wine and beer went down well and Simon being Simon kept on replacing the empties with full ones, and they all went through their own actions of the last few days, but he never mentioned the red wine in the bath.

It was getting too dark to try to find the caravan, so they all carried on drinking. As the evening went on the conversation became more and more comical, and the laughter louder as more and more alcohol was consumed.

They were oblivious to the outside changing environment as nightfall truly set in.

The last time they were here, they were literally fighting for their lives. It seemed a different lifetime ago.

"See, I told you we had secret passages here" Simon said with pride. "What! Never" Caelan said as the remainder laughed and pointed to the wood panel that Joe and Julia had seen George enter through; Joe remembered hitting his friend and hoped he was OK no matter what he had done.

Joe became more withdrawn from the conversation as his guilt came back to haunt him. The guilt of losing his three friends in Afghanistan, to meeting Julia, leaving the Army, the fate of his sister, coming to Simon and Jane's, raising the pistol to Julia's head, hitting George and of course the red wine incident. He couldn't forget, but he knew now, there was always another way, and he knew he would never try to harm Julia again. He also knew he would never be able to tell her how desperate he had become. It would never happen again.

THE STAND-OFF

The next morning, there were some very sore heads sitting feeling sorry for themselves around the table. Joe was glad he had stopped drinking earlier than the rest, but he also knew they had needed to let their hair down in order to at least try to feel human again.

The fresh air against Joe's face was a reminder of his love of the outdoors, in all of this mayhem, as he wandered up to the deer wood to check out the caravan they had installed for them; the wood had been named by Simon and Jane due to their small herd of fallow deer that roamed the hillside.

He sat on a rock and listened to the noise of the wood, with the singing of the birds under the rooftop canopy of the trees and the slow brushing wind passing through the branches. He missed the freedom it offered and for once, and for a short time, he felt free again; free from the pain and suffering he had brought to everyone he knew.

He eventually found the caravan which had been placed on the extreme edge of the wood far from anyone wandering through. Simon had done a great job of setting it up with its own temporary gas and water supply. The cupboards had also been filled with food and the fridge, with Simon's normal approach, had wine and beer as well as cold meats from the farm shop.

Joe could never repay what they had done for them, and they were all in this because of him. Even Caelan had been dragged into this but had become a good friend now, always there and never letting them down.

He sat in the caravan knowing he had to deal with his own guilt issues at some point, but also wishing he could do something to show how grateful he was to them all, every one of them. More importantly to Julia, the woman who had shown complete love for him throughout. She had never questioned his loyalty to her, and because of that he now needed to dedicate the rest of his life to loving her, showing her the love she had been neglected for many years.

He slowly wandered back to the farm feeling better about himself, and as he left the edge of the wood and could see the farm further down the track he looked around at the stunning, rolling countryside, as the sun was beginning to shine through the clouds onto the green fields, he could feel the warmth of the day on his face.

As he approached the main house he had an odd feeling that something wasn't right. He stopped by the corner of the building and drew his weapon. He slowly moved towards the window as he kept his back against the wall. He positioned himself at the bottom of the window and peeked through. The kitchen appeared to be empty so he moved past the window and towards the door. All the time he was checking the farm-yard and surrounding buildings for movement. It seemed all too quiet, and he had the feeling that trouble was around the corner.

He placed his hand on the handle of the door and slowly started to open it. He stopped the door after opening it an inch to check for booby-traps, as he had done so many times before on active service. He slowly opened the door enough for him to crouch and see in the room, the pistol always remaining at the ready. It was still too quiet.

He moved across the kitchen remaining at the same level as the work surfaces to the door at the opposite side, which led to the living room. The door was slightly open allowing Joe to peer through.

"Please come and join us, Joe" a muffled voice said before he got a chance to have any clear vision of those inside.

Joe pushed the door open and aimed his pistol at one of the six masked figures standing over Simon, Jane, Caelan and Julia, tied in their chairs with their mouths taped.

He was tempted to immediately start shooting but realised that all of the attacker's weapons were aimed at the hostages. If he fired, they would all be dead within seconds.

"Joe, let me explain why we are here and you can then make the decision as to what you want to do next."

Joe stayed silent, but still aiming the pistol.

"OK, here is the deal. Drop your weapon and we will let your friends go."

"Fucking no chance!"

Joe knew that they would all be killed no matter what happened once he lowered his weapon.

"Let me tell you how this is going to end. Untie them all and let them go, and I will come with you."

Julia started to shake her head.

"I don't think that's an option here Joe."

"Baby trust me. This is the best thing for you all" Joe said hoping his love would understand what he was about to do.

Joe knew he had to make a move, and soon. He had to think fast. "Let me make the decision easier for you."

Simon was pulled from his chair and thrown on the floor in front of the gunman. The masked, unknown assailant took aim and shot Simon through the leg. The bullet shattered his shinbones and blood splattered across the floor.

Simon could be heard screaming through the duct-tape as he wriggled in agony.

Joe took the shot and killed the gunman standing over Julia, took the second shot at the leader and caught him in the chest and the force pushed him back against the fireplace.

The remaining gunman started shooting in Joe's direction and he managed to shoot another in the throat before moving back behind the security of the stone kitchen wall.

The brickwork started crumbling as the rounds tried to find their target. Joe took another shot and could hear someone fall. He stood up and moved in full view of the remaining standing gunmen.

Joe felt the first round enter his stomach as he terminated the shooter, and went to take aim at the last standing gunman. He was again hit in his upper chest. Joe fell to the floor as the gunman started kicking the defenceless hostages to the floor from their chairs and taking aim and shooting them one by one.

He knew he had to stop him and, although his vision was blurring, he managed to aim only after the gunman had shot Julia through the back. Joe fired, took aim and shot him in the chest and stomach as he dropped behind where Julia lay.

Joe crawled towards Julia in agony and managed to remove the tape from her mouth. Blood was coming from her mouth and he could hear the sucking of the wound she had sustained in her back, and could feel the warmth of the blood against his chest. Joe propped her up and hugged her.

"I am so sorry, baby, I really am" he said as Julia started spluttering her words.

"I love you Joe, I always have. At least we are together to the end."

"Keep still baby, I love you."

Joe heard movement from the back of the room.

He turned his head to see the leader struggle to his feet and take aim at them both. Joe didn't initially seem to find the strength to take aim at him, but used all his force to allow him to take control one last time.

"Not this time!"

Joe raised the gun and whispered one last time to Julia the words he had said so many times since the night they had first been together.

"I love you, my beautiful baby."

He pulled the trigger, hoping this time the round would find its target and for their nightmare to be over once and for all.

The bullet entered the chest passing through the vital organs and killing the last of the masked attackers instantly. His body slid to the floor whilst his blood spread across the wooden oak beams of the ceiling and flowed across the stone, cold slabs of the floor away from his body.

Joe slumped next to Julia's body knowing he had fallen in love in an instant, loved since and will throughout eternity.

Their bodies lay on the blood-soaked floor, hearing again, the distant sirens of the emergency services on their way to either help, or to finish off the job their attackers had failed to achieve. Only time now would tell if they lived or died.

Love never dies, it only grows with time. It can mean having the strength to live or die with the person destiny has chosen for you to spend the rest of your life with. Love conquers all and there is nowhere to run from true love.